THE LAST GREEN FLASH

A Collection of Short Stories

MICHAEL PALMER

authorHOUSE®

AuthorHouse™
1663 Liberty Drive
Bloomington, IN 47403
www.authorhouse.com
Phone: 833-262-8899

Published by AuthorHouse 02/24/2023

ISBN: 978-1-6655-7981-0 (sc)
ISBN: 978-1-6655-7980-3 (e)

Library of Congress Control Number: 2023900635

Blueberry Hill
Words and Music by AL LEWIS, VINCENT ROSE and LARRY STOCK
• 1940 (Renewed) CHAPPELL & CO., INC., LARRY STOCK
MUSIC CO. (c/o LARRY SPIER MUSIC, LLC) and
SOVEREIGN MUSIC CO.
All Rights Reserved
Used by Permission of ALFRED MUSIC

Blueberry Hill
Words and Music by Al Lewis, Larry Stock and Vincent Rose
Copyright © 1940 Chappell & Co., Inc., Larry Stock Music,
Larry Spier Music LLC and Sovereign Music
Corp. Copyright Renewed
All Rights for Larry Stock Music and Larry Spier Music LLC Administered
by Downtown Music Services All Rights Reserved Used by Permission
Reprinted by Permission of Hal Leonard LLC

Print information available on the last page.

This book is printed on acid-free paper.

Because of the dynamic nature of the Internet, any web addresses or links contained in this book may have changed since publication and may no longer be valid. The views expressed in this work are solely those of the author and do not necessarily reflect the views of the publisher, and the publisher hereby disclaims any responsibility for them.

DEDICATION

This work is dedicated to my father, who was an inspiration for me throughout his lifetime. He inspired me to challenge myself and to also take time to enjoy the splendor of the green flash. Whenever I see that burst of green, I think of him.

ACKNOWLEDGEMENTS

This book would not be possible without the help
and encouragement of many people.

First, I would like to thank those friends who read many
of my short stories and were helpful in pointing out
numerous errors and offering suggestions. Tom Buchman,
Nancy Leavenworth, and June Craner, thank you.

Thanks to Peter Davidson for his valuable advice on publishing
and for leading me in the direction of AuthorHouse.

I also wish to thank Robert Jackson for the many hours he spent
editing and proofing this manuscript. Bob, you have done a
masterful job, but, of course, any remaining errors fall on me.

To Eve Ardell and Annie Barrete at AuthorHouse who
patiently guided me through the submission and publication
process and whose involvement made this book a reality.

To the copyright holders of the lyrics to Blueberry Hill, thanks for
giving me permission to use the song in my story, Fats Domino.

Finally, I wish to thank my wife, Charmaine, for the
encouragement to do something during the COVID-19
pandemic other than watching television. Without your
gentle pushing I'd still be watching Seinfeld reruns.

CONTENTS

PARTY LINES

THE PHONE RANG. TWO RINGS, followed by a pause, then another two rings.

"Don't answer that Keith. Its not ours."

It was my mom reminding me not to answer when it was two rings. That was the Smith's ring.

It was 1950. We lived in Ireton, Iowa. Named after Henry Ireton, an English general in the parliamentary army during the English Civil War. The son-in-law of Oliver Cromwell and the signer of the death warrant for King Charles I. Population 573, although my dad said they must have double counted.

Ireton, Iowa, where phones were party lines, where we shared a single line with other homes, and in our case with Mr. and Mrs. Smith.

During and after World War II the telephone lines were expensive and not readily available. This was especially true in rural areas where we lived. Like us, many families could only afford to have a phone if it was a party line.

Since we shared a phone line with the Smiths, they could pick up the phone and listen to our conversations. Of course, we could do the same. And when my parents weren't home, I did.

It was a rotary phone. A brand new one too. Shiny black, metal, with a faceplate showing numbers and letters. A prominent wheel on the faceplate, with ten holes, each just large enough for a fingertip to spin the wheel clockwise to the finger stop. And finally, it's large handset with the earpiece at one end and the speaking piece at the other, resting in its cradle atop the phone.

My parents were so proud of our new Western Electric 302 rotary phone. It even had a special place on the tall side table in the living room. I suspected they put it there so any visitor would easily notice it and, of course, admire their prize possession.

There were certain rules, unwritten of course, when it came to the phone. Limit your time on the phone. Do not dial if the phone is in use. Hang up if the other party has an emergency call to make. And, of course, don't listen in to the other party's conversation.

School was out for the summer. Kids were up to their usual shenanigans; one was listening in on party line conversations. I was no exception.

Dad was at work and mom was visiting a friend in the next town. We had no television, although dad said it would be the next big purchase after he had the car repaired. We had a large bulky radio, which we would gather around in the evening. The Lone Ranger was my favorite. Lawrence Welk, and the champagne bubbles, not so much. So, the only entertainment in the afternoon was playing with my dog Tippy, and you guessed it, eavesdropping on the party line.

The phone rang. Two rings. It was for the Smiths. An older couple. Mr. Smith, a traveling salesman, was on the road most of the time. Some said he had a mistress in Illinois, others said it was his nagging wife. My dad said it was probably both. But whatever, he was gone a lot.

I waited for about a minute. Then slowly, ever so carefully, I picked up the heavy headset and put it to my ear, remembering to clamp one hand over the mouthpiece so I wouldn't be heard.

"Do you think it's possible?" It was Mr. Smith's voice. Rough and hoarse. Just like his personality. Scary as well and not much for jokes. It was no wonder that their house was one to avoid on Halloween night.

"If you have the money, anything is possible," was the reply from an unrecognized man.

"I need to think about it."

"I understand, but don't think too long as my offer is only good for 24 hours."

"Why is that? Only 24 hours?"

"Because I need to leave town after."

"Oh, you're that busy?"

"Yeah, you wouldn't believe how many husbands are ready to do what you want. Some wives too."

"Jesus, I had no idea."

"And of course, they all want it hush hush. They certainly don't want to arouse any suspicion."

"No, no, I don't want that. It must seem natural. Not suspicious."

"And that's why you've contacted me."

"Yes, your number was given to me by an out-of-town acquaintance. Said you were one of the best."

"Oh?"

"Yes, by someone I know in Illinois."

"Name?"

"Sorry, I told the lady ... er, person, I wouldn't involve them in this matter. Too messy you know."

"Well yes, it usually is. Potentially very messy. But then again, it depends on how you want it done."

"Of course, how it's done. I assume we can discuss that?"

"If you want to, we can, but most clients would rather not know. They leave that up to me."

"Yes, I can imagine not wanting to know how it will happen."

"Yeah, most think it's better not to know, at least in advance."

"Give me 24 hours to think about it. Can you call tomorrow at this time? My wife has an appointment and will not be here."

"Sure thing. Tomorrow. Bye."

"Bye."

There was a click as the call was disconnected. Then silence. I slowly slid the handset back into its cradle.

Jesus, I thought, what was that all about? What was Mr. Smith planning? A very mysterious conversation. Very mysterious indeed.

The rest of my day was uneventful, although I kept thinking about the conversation. Words and phrases like "messy, suspicious, leaving town right after, better not to know" were circling in my head. And what did this have to do with a lady in Illinois? Was that Mr. Smith's girlfriend? Was she part of his plans?

Then there was the question of whether I should tell anyone. My mother, my father? They would probably be upset with me for listening in. They might make me apologize to Mr. Smith. Oh Jesus, they probably would do that. And the police, how could I go to them? What would I tell them? They'd probably think another bored kid pulling a prank on them.

That night I hardly slept. Tossing and turning. Not sure what to do. And anxious for the follow up phone call. Anxious, yet terrified.

Dad was off to work, his general store needed restocking, and mom had decided to spend another afternoon with her friend. It was just Tippy and me when the phone rang at 1:00 o'clock. Exactly at 1 o'clock, two rings, then a pause, just like yesterday.

I reached for the handset, but my hand was not steady. The handset bumped up against the phone as I picked it up. My heart leaped to my throat.

"What was that, that noise?" The man's voice boomed in the earpiece. I held my breath.

"What noise?" It was Mr. Smith. "I didn't hear anything."

"Do you have a party line?"

"Yes, but I wouldn't worry. They follow the rules."

"I just want to make sure. I don't want anyone knowing about what I'm about to do."

"Of course, of course."

"So, what have you decided!"

"Yes, I want you to do it."

"Okay, but you have to pay me in advance,"

"Oh?"

"Yes, the full amount in advance and in cash. Is there a problem with that?"

"Oh no, no problem. I'll go to the bank this afternoon. I assume it's the amount we discussed earlier?"

"Yes, that's the amount, and remember in cash. Cash only."

"No problem."

"So, does tonight work for you?"

"Yes, that will work."

"Will she be home? I mean it's important that she be there."

"Oh yes, she will. The unsuspecting victim will."

Mr. Smith let out a loud, long laugh. The man at the other end remained silent.

"8:00 tonight then, after it's dark will be best."

"And the mess, what about the mess?"

"Leave that to me. I know how to take care of the mess."

"Thank goodness, I was hoping you would. Not sure I could do it."

"Don't worry Mr. Smith. No one will see any difference after I'm finished. Not even you. Like nothing ever happened. I mean that's what you want. Right?"

"God yes."

"Okay, it's set for tonight night then. I'll come by for the money later today. Remember, cash only."

"Hey, just one other thing."

"What?"

"I don't even know your name. What should I call you?"

"Is that important, Mr. Smith? I don't think so if I do what I say I'm going to do."

"Yes, I guess so."

"Tonight, unless you change your mind and don't want me to do it. Of course, if you do change your mind, the money is still mine."

"I'm not changing my mind. I've been thinking about this for years and now I have the nerve to do it."

"Okay, bye for now."

"Bye."

I stood there, silently, holding the phone, dark thoughts racing through my head. Jesus, what was going on.

Then I heard a voice.

"Hey, is someone on this line? Is that you Mrs. Wells."

I held my breath. I looked at Tippy. Please don't bark, I mouthed.

"Keith, is that you? Are you on the other line?"

Say nothing, perhaps he'll hang up. That's all I could think of.

After what seemed like eternity, Mr. Smith hung up. I put the handset down and let out a loud sigh of relief.

At dinner that evening, I could hardly eat.

"Is everything ok, Keith? You're not eating much." It was my mom. She had prepared my favorite meal. Hamburgers and French fries. I even had a Coke to drink.

"Er, okay. Everything's okay. Just thinking about tonight's Lone Ranger radio show."

"Well don't forget Lawrence Welk," my dad said with a chuckle.

"No dad, how could I forget."

I nibbled at my hamburger. It was cold now. I wanted to tell my parents what I had heard, but I was afraid to. What if Mr. Smith figured out it was me on the party line? What would he do? What would he ask that man to do?

The Lone Ranger and Tonto. A brand-new story, but I hardly listened. I kept thinking of tonight at 8 o'clock. Lawrence Welk came on, it was just 8 o'clock. The time they had agreed to. The mess, I kept thinking of the mess and cleaning up so no one would notice.

I quickly rose to my feet.

"I'm not feeling too good. I'm going to my room."

As I left, I glanced at the phone. Jesus, why did I have to listen in?"

"Okay, rest up, big day tomorrow. First day of the fall term. You want to be awake for school."

Big day, I thought, as I got in bed. Bigger night tonight, that's for sure. I covered my head with the pillow, but I could still hear Lawrence Welk, that familiar "and a one and a two ..." Damn bubbles, I thought, as I tried to fall asleep.

There was a knock at my door.

"Keith, time to get up. Breakfast in 30 minutes." It was mom. She sounded so cheerful. If only she knew.

The table was set. Dad having coffee and my cereal bowl was full of Rice Krispies. Mom was pouring in the milk. The snap, crackle and pop startled me. I had been thinking about how he did it. How the man took care of Mrs. Smith. Broke her neck? Shot her? God, did I really want to know.

The phone rang. Just one ring. It was for us.

Mom got up, went into the other room, and answered. After a few minutes, she returned to the table. I noticed her look of surprise. She wanted to say something but couldn't find the words. The right words. Finally,

"You're not going to believe what happened to Mrs. Smith last night."

"What?" dad asked.

"Unbelievable. Who would have thought? Here in Ireton, Iowa."

"What, what happened, Sylvia?"

"I just can't believe it, Earl. What happened."

"What? What?" My dad was shouting now, coffee was sloshing out of his cup.

"It must have been a real mess." Mom was shaking her head back and forth. "A real mess."

"Mess? Sylvia, what do you mean?"

"It was their 50th anniversary and Mr. Smith paid some guy to jump out of a big cake."

"Really?" Dad started laughing.

"Yes, really and the guy … the guy was practically naked! And Mrs. Smith fainted. Fainted and fell headlong into the cake. Can you believe it, Earl? Can you believe it?"

"God, what a mess. I can just picture it now. Cake and frosting everywhere. Poor Mrs. Smith. Imagine she had to clean up that mess after."

Before I could stop myself, I spoke up, "but she didn't have to clean up."

My parents looked at me and at the same time said, "What did you say."

I looked down at my breakfast. My cereal was cold and soggy. No more popping or snapping. Still, I ate it.

"Naked coming out of a cake! Jesus, I wish I had been there," my dad said.

And then mom, "Oh yes, that would have been something to see, the look on Mrs. Smith's face."

"What do you think, Keith?'

I said nothing. Didn't really want to, but then I thought perhaps I had been wrong about Mr. Smith all this time and that next Halloween I would stop at their house.

MY GRANDPARENTS

IT WAS A SMALL APARTMENT. The kitchen, dining room, and living room, consisted of a single open space. A bathroom with its small black and white tile floor, and a bedroom, which looked out onto a metal fire escape. That was their apartment. My grandparents.

On the third floor of a four-story red brick apartment building built in 1929. Apartment 3C. Overlooking Barnes Avenue below, where kids would play stick ball, while avoiding the random automobile. Across the street the St. Thomas Catholic Church, where rumor had it that my grandfather slipped away one afternoon to have me baptized.

It was one of our many trips down to the city to visit my grandparents. About an hour's drive along the Hudson River from upstate New York, where we lived. It would also be our last trip to the city, and we all knew it.

They were sitting at the kitchen table and preparing the wine to drink. My grandfather and my dad. Cutting oranges into slices, to add a sweet fruity twist to the dark red chianti wine. Occasionally, my dad would dip his finger in his glass and let me taste it. Even though I was three years short of ten, I felt so grown up when he did.

Dinner was over. A meat dish, chicken, followed by spaghetti, with meatballs. Ice cream for dessert. It was time for the cigars.

My grandfather loved his cigar after dinner. My dad too. They were Toscano cigars, imported from Italy. My grandfather would only smoke these cigars. "From the rolling hills of Tuscany," he would say in his broken English.

The cigar ritual fascinated me. Long wooden matches were always used. Then they would hold their cigars between their fingers, rolling it ever so slowly so that the entire end met the dancing flame. Once lit, they would gently blow on the ash to control the burning. And finally, the first few, small, quick puffs, before the actual smoking.

The smell of cigar smoke filled the room. I loved that smell. I can still smell it now when I think about that apartment. That thick, heavy, sweet smell of a burning cigar. A Toscano cigar.

With their backs to the table, grandma and my mother were at the kitchen sink doing the dishes. They weren't speaking. I often wondered if they didn't care for one another. Perhaps my grandmother wanted her son, John to marry an Italian girl. Instead, he fell in love with a German girl, Edna Anna. I was their first child, Michael.

It was the 1940s and it was in the heart of the east Bronx in New York City. A few blocks away the elevated train, known as the Bronx El, crawled noisily above 3rd Avenue. For 15 cents one could travel from lower Manhattan to the Bronx.

The steel infrastructure which supported the El, cast the neighborhood below in perpetual darkness.

In the Bronx, life above and below the El, was depressing. The tracks almost touched the old apartment buildings, with the noise and the dirt affecting the tenants 24 hours a day. Business below tended to be low rent places, like pawn brokers, bars, cigar shops, and newsstands.

But a few blocks away, on the corner of 221st and Barnes, where my grandparents lived, it was a different world. The sun shone and the quiet neighborhood was only disturbed by the occasional ice truck delivering 20 to 40-pound blocks of ice to those who still had iceboxes. The iceman, as he was called, would use a pair of tongs to lift the block of ice onto his back and carry it to those apartments whose tenants had placed an "Ice Today" card in their window. Yes, it was a different world from that above and below the noisy dirty El, whose 80-year run would come to an end in the mid1950s.

My grandfather, who served in the Italian Army at the turn of the century, immigrated from southern Italy to the United States in the early 1900s. Like most immigrants of that time, he came to America in search of making a living. Times were difficult in Italy.

A barber by trade, he set up his own barber shop in the Bronx shortly after his arrival. The Modern Barber Shop, as it was called. It also had an adjacent room where my grandmother tended to women's hair.

My father and I never went to the Modern Barber Shop. We never had to. On almost every visit to the apartment on 121st street, my grandfather would take out his barber tools and cut our hair in the middle of the small living room. He would finish our haircuts, by taking a small flame to our newly cut hair to "seal the ends."

My grandmother, who was born in the city, was usually in the background of her husband. Unassuming, she accepted her outwardly lesser role, like most Italian married women of that time. But it was clear that she was much stronger than her appearance would suggest. I often thought she called the shots in their relationship.

Grandma was a wonderful cook. Anything Italian. And one could never leave her table hungry. "Mangiare, mangiare," she would say, "eat, eat," as she filled my plate for the second time with her spaghetti. And, of course, I never protested.

While my grandfather drank his wine, my grandmother had her coffee. I often wondered if she enjoyed coffee or was it simply the taste of the copious amounts of condensed milk and sugar she added to the cup.

It was getting dark outside. It was Sunday night. It was almost time to leave.

Our goodbyes were different this time. Long hugs. We were leaving in a few days for California.

I didn't know it at the time, but it would be the last time I would see him. My grandfather. The last time I would watch him prepare his wine, light his cigar, or give me a haircut.

As we were leaving, my grandfather slumped onto the couch in front of his new television. A gift from my dad. There was a special on TV. Italy. I looked at my grandfather. Tears swelled in his eyes. I waved goodbye.

The final ride home seemed longer than usual. I sat in the back, wondering if my grandfather was crying because he missed Italy, or because I was leaving. I didn't ask, but I wanted to think it was the latter.

CRICKETS

THE CRICKETS WERE CHIRPING. As it grew darker, their sounds grew louder. The males were on the prowl for a mate.

Sitting outside on the back deck, I turned to Charlie. I had just finished my second can of Budweiser.

"What are you up for?"

"Shit, I don't know. Any suggestions?"

"A movie?"

"No way. We did that last week."

"Well, that was last week."

"And we hated it, remember. Even the popcorn was stale."

"Ok, want to hit the bars?"

"Like the crickets?"

"What? Crickets?"

"Yeah, they're on the hunt tonight."

"Are you suggesting we head to the bars and make chirping noises?"

"Actually, it's from rubbing the edges of their wings together."

"Sure, wings, where are we going to get wings?"

"Oh, come on, maybe it'll be our lucky night."

The taxi dropped us off in front of the Pioneer Bar. A local hangout for singles and those who wanted to be, at least for the evening.

There was no line at the front door and the bouncer looked bored.

"Slow night?" I asked him.

Standing well over six foot, he looked down at me. Arms crossed, muscles bulging. While dark sunglasses concealed his eyes, his smile suggested I had asked him a dumb question.

"You think?" He replied with a southern drawl.

"Do you need to see identification?" Charlie asked.

Without answering, he simply waved us by.

As we entered the venue, I turned to Charlie.

"Friendly guy, huh?"

"You think?"

There was a light crowd. The band was in the process of setting up. We moved to two empty seats at the far end of the bar.

"What ya all drinking?" It was the bartender. She was smiling. A young girl, blonde, shapely, and certainly more friendly than the front door bouncer.

"A Bud Light," Charlie replied.

"Make that two," I said.

"Watching your waistlines?" She said with a delightful laugh.

"Can't be too careful?" I replied holding in my stomach.

As she left to get our beer, Charlie tapped me on my shoulder.

"You can exhale now. She's gone."

The band was finished with their warmup, so they started their set. Electric guitars and drums blasted through the bar. One singer with a booming voice adding to the ear-piercing decibel level.

"Hardly dancing music," Charlie shouted.

"I doubt anyone's here to dance."

"Two Bud Lights." She was back. "And here's some peanuts."

"Thanks, sweetheart." I replied as she walked away.

Charlie nudged me. Twice.

"She's a little young, don't you think?"

I just shrugged my shoulders and reached for the peanuts.

The bar was about half full. A few patrons were dancing on the floor in front of the band platform.

Two girls were sitting at the other end of the bar. They were giggling and whispering in each other's ears.

"What about those two," Charlie said nodding furiously in their direction.

"Could you be a little more obvious, Charlie?"

"I wanted them to see me. I wanted to show them that we were interested."

"Where did you hear about that pick-up strategy?"

"Nowhere, just figured I'd try it."

The two girls suddenly smiled at us. Perhaps Charlie was on to something, but of course I would never tell him that.

"Look, look they acknowledged us."

Charlie was so excited that he knocked over my beer. The foamy liquid eased its way down the top of the bar.

"Christ Charlie, calm down. You would think a young girl had never smiled at you before."

"Damn it, we should buy them some drinks. "Whata you think?"

"Hey guys, can't hold your Bud Light?" It was the bartender. She was headed our way, wiping the bar with a towel as she approached.

"My friend here just got overly excited."

"At what?"

I didn't know what to say, but of course Charlie didn't hold back.

"Those two girls at the other end of the bar, we'd like to buy them a round. And peanuts too."

"Sure, but you know the peanuts are free, right?"

"Yeah, but give them some extra."

"Whatever you say, big spender."

The bartender walked to the other end of the bar. Although we couldn't hear her, we assumed she was telling the two girls that we were buying them a round. Hopefully she didn't mention the peanuts.

The two smiled, waved and nodded thank you.

"We're in," Charlie whispered.

"Not so fast, Charlie. Let's see how this plays out."

The girls finished their drinks and held up their empty glasses. They tilted their heads, as if asking for more. Of course, Charlie couldn't resist.

"Bartender, another round for our friends at the end of the bar," he shouted.

And so, the evening progressed. We with our Bud Lights at one end of the bar and our two acquaintances at the other end running up our tab.

"I think it's time we made our move." Charlie said, easing himself off his bar stool. "Come on."

Beer bottles in hand, we worked our way around the occupied bar stools to the other end of the bar. Charlie was taking the lead as he always did.

"Good evening, ladies."

"Hi."

"Enjoying your drinks?"

"Well, yes, thank you."

I thought of asking them about the extra peanuts, but decided just to observe Charlie at work.

"Nice evening."

"Well, yes, it is."

"I'm Charlie, and this is my roommate, Mike."

"Nice to meet you."

"Might you two be interested in finding a quieter place to drink?"

"Huh?"

"There's a nice lounge in the hotel across the street."

"Sorry, but …"

"Or we could just stay here. Whatever suits you."

"Sorry, if we mislead you, but…"

"Oh, you're a couple?"

"No, but we're waiting for our boyfriends."

"Boyfriends?"

"We just thought you two were being nice to us and wanted to buy us drinks."

We just stood there. Not sure how to respond. I decided to break the awkward silence.

"Yes, of course, that was what we were doing. Come on Charlie, let's move along. It's getting late and we need to get back."

The cab door shut with a dull thud. Charlie turned to me.

"Jesus, what was that all about? I didn't see that coming. And did you see their bar tab? What the hell were they drinking? Dom Perignon champagne?"

"Peanuts."

"What?"

"It must have been the extra peanuts. Drove up the bar bill."

The taxi came to a stop. We were home.

As the taxi door opened, I heard the crickets. Their chirping was as loud as before.

"I hope they were luckier than we were."

Walking towards the building's entrance, I grabbed on to Charlie's arm.

"Too many beers, Mike?"

The two large doors opened, and we entered the lobby. Barbara was sitting behind the welcome counter.

"Good evening, gentlemen. Big night out?"

"Yeah Barb."

"What did you do? Hit the bars again?"

"Yep."

"I won't ask."

"No need, same results."

"Well, I have to give you credit for trying."

"Yeah."

"I mean, you're the only two guys in this retirement home that even go out at night. And both in your 80s, who would believe it."

As I reached for my walking cane which had slipped to the lobby floor, I looked up and replied,

"I guess we're just two old crickets, nothing to show for it but loud chirping."

OUR LAST HIKE IN THE WOODS

There were just four of us. Young kids on a hike in the woods. Saturday morning. Early spring.

Gang of Four, our parents called us. Each an only kid, two guys and two girls, ten to twelve in ages. The best of friends.

The new leaves above us were bursting forth with the arrival of the spring rains. The air had a smell of freshness and newness.

The woods were waking from a long, cold winter.

I loved being out here with my three best friends. We did everything together and we told each other everything, even things that were best left a secret. But that's what best friends do.

Nancy, June, Yoshi, and me. The Gang of Four.

We approached the river where we would always stop. Then find our favorite spot, that grassy knoll at the edge of the river, where we would sit and talk and have the snacks our moms prepared for us.

"Peanut butter and jelly," Nancy shouted. "Me too." It was June.

"A cheese sandwich for me." I was holding my sandwich above my head like I had just won a prize.

"What about you, Yoshi?"

Yoshi didn't answer. He was looking at the fast-flowing river. His back was to the three of us.

"Yoshi, what did your mom make for you?" It was June. Nancy and

I thought she had a crush on Yoshi. June said she didn't, but then she smiled, and we said, "sure."

Yoshi still didn't say anything. He picked up a stick and threw it into the river. As it disappeared downstream, he turned.

"Nothing. My mom didn't have time this morning."

"Here," June jumped to her feet, "I can share."

Nancy looked at me and smiled. I just shrugged my shoulders in return. Yes, there was a crush. A definite crush.

"No, that's okay. I'm not hungry." Yoshi looked back at the raging river and reached for another stick.

"What's wrong, Yoshi, you've been so quiet all morning. It's not like you." It was Nancy now.

Yes indeed, it was not like him. Yoshi was usually the most talkative of the gang. Keeping all of us in stitches with his stories, mainly of his dad's business. The Nishimura Laundry. The small laundry in the town of Bodega Bay, in Northern California, where we all lived.

Yoshi told us stories of the things that people would bring in for cleaning. Mrs. Scott with her husband's worn-out bedroom slippers. All she had of her husband after he ran away with his secretary. Not sure why she wanted to keep them, Mr. Nishimura would say. But he always took extra care in cleaning them.

Mr. Brown with his old baseball hat. "Worn by Babe Ruth," he would boast. Of course, Yoshi's dad never told him it was a Brooklyn Dodgers hat and that the Babe never played for them. No way, it would have ruined the story and would probably be bad for business. The stories never stopped, except for today.

"Cat got your tongue, Yoshi?" I joined the group expressing concern.

"Just not in the mood, I guess." Yoshi finally replied, as another stick made its way downstream.

"Come on, Yoshi, this is not like you? What's bothering you. You can tell us."

After a few minutes of silence and more airborne sticks, Yoshi turned to the three of us. I could tell he had been quietly crying. He wiped the tears from his swollen eyes. Then he started telling us.

"Last night. Dad... Dad told me we had... to leave Bodega Bay."

"What?" The three of us jumped to our feet and screamed almost at the same time.

"Why, are you moving?" It was June. I sensed a tone of anguish in her voice.

"We don't want to," Yoshi said, looking down at the new grass. "We have to."

The three of us stood there, each trying to understand what Yoshi had just told us. It made no sense. Had to leave? After a while he continued.

"All the Japanese, we must leave. The government said so." A fresh pool of tears filled his eyes.

"But why? I don't understand." It was June again and she looked like she was about to cry as well.

"I don't know. My dad didn't tell me. He just said be ready to leave next week."

"But where are you going?" June was crying now.

"I don't know. Dad doesn't know. We just must be ready to leave. He gave me a small suitcase and said that's all I could take, whatever I could get in it."

"What, a small suitcase? That's all?" Now I was asking questions.

"Nothing else, that's what dad said."

"But what about Koda?"

Koda was Yoshi's dog. A Japanese Akita.

His grandmother brought Koda with her when she came to Bodega Bay from Japan. All the way on a big ship. All the way with Koda. I thought back to that day, now long ago, when Mr. and Mrs. Nishimura and Yoshi drove down to San Francisco to meet her ship. And they all came back with Koda.

Koda. All the kids in the neighborhood loved Koda. Big and lovable, like a teddy bear.

Yoshi burst out with loud sobs. He was shaking all over.

"Dad said ... he said, Koda will have to stay. I can't take him."

"No, no, that can't be," Nancy was shouting. "What will happen to Koda?"

Yoshi shook his head. "Dad said we'll try to find him a home. A good home."

I walked over to Yoshi and put my hands on his shoulders. "I'll take him, I'll take Koda. I'll give him a good home, and when you return, he'll be waiting for you." Now I was crying. Yoshi said nothing.

"What about the house and the laundry?" June asked. "What will happen to those?"

"Dad is trying to sell them, but so far, no one is interested. So, I guess we're leaving them too."

The rest of the early afternoon we just sat there, on the banks of the river. We hardly spoke, probably because we didn't know what to say and we certainly didn't understand what was happening. Why Yoshi had to leave.

It was starting to get cold when we decided to walk back to Bodega Bay. As we entered the sleepy town on the Pacific coast, we passed the hospital. The Bodega Bay Hospital, where Yoshi would always tell us when we passed, "that's where I was born, room 312." We were all born in that hospital.

We were in the center of town now. The Nishimura Laundry was in sight. We stopped just in front. The store was all boarded up. A For Sale sign was taped to the front door. There was another sign, in bold dark letters, a notice, dated May 10, 1942. I walked up to it and started to read out loud.

"Instructions to all persons of Japanese Ancestry living in the area of Bodega Bay, California. Pursuant to the provisions of the Civilian Exclusion Order, all persons of Japanese ancestry, both alien and non-alien, will be evacuated from this area by 12 o'clock noon, Saturday May 16,1942."

I stopped and scanned down the document when I saw it.

"No pets of any kind will be permitted."

There were more instructions. Many more. But I continued to stare at "no pets ..."

Then my gaze shifted to another large piece of plywood covering the front window. Someone had painted on the wood. The letters were so big, I had to step back to read them

REMEMBER PEARL HARBOR
JAPS GO HOME

We were all overwhelmed. The three of us turned to Yoshi who was crying uncontrollably now. The three of us started crying too.

I looked at Yoshi, he looked back.

I turned and looked at the painted words, and then in between my sobs, I shouted. I shouted as loud as I could. I wanted everyone to hear me. Everyone in Bodega Bay.

"This is his home. Damn it. This is Yoshi's home."

YOSHI RETURNS

IT WAS A SUNNY MORNING in Bodega Bay. Hot too. A typical August day. What was not typical were the flags. Every home in the town displayed a flag. Some on flag poles, most in windows.

"The stars and stripes," my dad said as he placed our flag in the front window.

The war was over. Japan had surrendered.

A parade was planned for the weekend.

"We need to show our support for the troops," my dad said," for their sacrifices," my mom added.

"But what about …" I started to ask. Before, I could finish my mom spoke up.

"Yes, our boys sacrificed so much."

"But what about …" this time my dad interrupted.

"That's why we're having this parade. To show our respects. And to welcome them home."

"What about you, Junior? Aren't you excited for this parade?"

Finally, at last my presence had been acknowledged.

"Yes, but …"

"But what, Junior?"

"What about Yoshi?" I shouted out his name. "When is he coming home?"

"Yoshi?" My mom and dad said his name at the same time.

"Yes, and his parents and his grandma. When are they coming home? Back to Bodega Bay?"

"Well, Junior, they never really left you know. They just spent some time away. I'm sure it was for the best, for them and for the country." My dad's voice rang hollow. I wasn't sure if he really believed what he was telling me. I wanted to believe he didn't. But I continued pushing.

"But this was their home, here in Bodega Bay, and they had to leave. They were told to leave."

Looking down at my side, I felt Koda against my leg. Memories of that day in front of the boarded-up Nishimura Laundry came rushing back. No pets permitted.

"And Yoshi had to leave Koda."

My parents said nothing. Were they embarrassed? Or perhaps they didn't know what to say? I reached down to pet Koda. Yoshi's dog, Koda.

The parade was long and loud. Almost everyone was there. I spent most of my time looking through the crowd for Yoshi. I wondered if I would recognize him after almost four years. Would he recognize me? I never saw him. I went home disappointed.

Weeks passed. Cool September replaced hot August. But still no Yoshi. I had almost given up hope of seeing my best friend, when there was phone call from Nancy. Her voice resonated with excitement.

"Have you heard?"

"Heard what Nancy?"

"Yoshi. He's back." She was almost shouting. I pictured her jumping up and down.

"Where?"

"Here in Bodega Bay. He's back."

I tried to speak, but I couldn't find the words. My breathing grew faster. Nancy's voice broke the silence.

"Did you hear me? Yoshi's back."

As my breathing slowed, I was able to reply.

"Where are they living?"

"Renting a room in their old house on Sycamore Street.

Oh yes, their house, on Sycamore Street. Former house. After they

THE LAST GREEN FLASH

left, the bank sold their home. New owners from San Francisco, tore up Mr. Nishimura's garden. Gone were those tasty Japanese eggplants.

"June and I are going over there today. Do you want to join us?"

"Of course. I'll meet you in front of their house. I'll bring Koda."

I was on Sycamore Street in front of the house. Pacing back and forth on the cracked sidewalk, with Koda at my side, glancing at my wristwatch about every minute. Then I saw them, Nancy, and June. It was 1:00 in the afternoon. I was annoyed.

"I thought you said to meet at noon?"

Nancy nodded in the direction of June and smiled. I knew with that smile not to continue my questioning. June simply wanted to look her best for Yoshi.

I knocked on the front door. There was no answer and we started walking away. But then, we heard the click of the lock.

As the door started to open, I moved forward. It was Yoshi's dad.

"Junior, Nancy, June how nice to see you."

He had lost weight and his once dark hair was grey. He held a cane in his hand to steady himself. Mrs. Nishimura waved at us from the hallway but didn't say anything. It looked like she had been crying.

"Is Yoshi here?"

"Yoshi. He went for a walk in the woods."

It was an uncomfortable moment, standing there at the open door. I didn't know what I should say. Mr. Nishimura recognizing my discomfort, came to my rescue,

"He said he was going to his favorite place, by the river. I'm sure you can find him there."

Before I could say thanks, the door closed.

Yoshi was there, sitting on the grassy knoll overlooking the river. His back was to us.

Koda barked and Yoshi spun around. Even after four years, Koda recognized him. Yoshi held out his hands and Koda leaped into them.

At last, The Gang of Four was together again. We had so many questions for Yoshi. At first, he was reluctant to answer, but eventually he did.

"Where did you go? Where did they take you?"

"Someplace in Wyoming. There was nothing there. Just the camp. And us, and the guards."

"Guards? What guards?"

"Soldiers with guns in towers watching us, night and day."

"What did you do?"

"Nothing."

"But you're back now." It was June, she was sitting next to him. Close, too.

"I guess," Yoshi replied, picking up a stick and tossing it into the river.

"What do you mean? You don't sound happy about being back."

"Yeah, we're back. Renting the basement of the house we once lived in. And my dad's laundry, now someone else owns it." The anger in his voice was obvious. I had never heard that before. It frightened me.

The three of us didn't know what to say. Finally, Nancy spoke up.

"But you have Koda. And you have us."

Yoshi didn't reply. Another stick went into the river.

"We saw your dad. How's your grandmother?"

"Don't know."

"Isn't she with you?"

"No."

"What happened?"

"She went back to Japan. The first ship she could take. Said she didn't want to die and be buried in this country. She wanted nothing to do with this country."

We sat in silence, again. Staring at the river. It didn't look the same to me. None of this looked, or felt the same. I tried to remember what it was like being here but couldn't. I wondered if it ever could be the same.

Yoshi stood up. He was much taller now. Taller than any of us.

"I must get back. Mom and dad are expecting me."

The walk back was difficult. Probably for all of us. I realized that the Gang of Four was no more. Too much time had passed and too much had happened. We could never be the same.

We walked with Yoshi to the front door. I wanted to give him a hug but felt he didn't want too. We simply shook hands. Nancy and June said nothing.

"Next week?" I said, "how about a hike next week."

"Sure. Give me about a week. I have to help mom and dad."

The door shut and Yoshi and Koda were gone.

A week later the three of us were back on Sycamore Street. June had even made a sandwich for Yoshi.

The new owners opened the door. "Can we help you?"

"We've come to see Yoshi."

They looked at one another, hoping that the other one would respond. Finally, the woman spoke.

"Yoshi's not here."

"Oh, when will he be back."

"I'm sorry, but they … they left this morning for San Francisco."

"San Francisco. Why did they go to San Francisco?"

"Well, they are going back to Japan. I'm sorry, didn't you know?"

I wanted to scream, or cry, or bang my fist against the door. But I just stood there. Behind me I could hear Nancy and June crying.

"But he did leave something for all of you. Something to remember him by, he said."

Staring at me from behind her was Koda. He had left Koda.

FATS DOMINO

THE CAR CAME TO A slow rolling stop. I parked in the perfect spot. The overlook atop Mount Soledad. Below were the lights of the city, San Diego. The half-moon reflected off the dark waters of the Pacific Ocean. An airplane, with its landing lights on, approached from the north.

And she was next to me. It was 1956.

The radio was on, and Fats Domino was singing. My favorite song, my favorite singer.

> *I found my thrill*
> *On Blueberry Hill*
> *On Blueberry Hill*
> *When I found you*

We had gone to dinner. Nothing fancy, of course. A pizza, cheese, no onion, and two Cokes. Then to a drive-in movie. I didn't make any moves there. We just enjoyed the movie. And after all it was a comedy. I thought later, yes later, I would make my move.

> *The moon stood still*
> *On Blueberry Hill*
> *And lingered until*
> *My dream came true*

I first saw her in my high school math class. That was last year. We were juniors. I was smitten. She was unaware. I spent so much time looking at her and dreaming about her in class that I barely got a C. She got an A.

The wind in the willow played
Love's sweet melody
But all of those vows you made
Were never to be

It took me a whole month before I got up the nerve to ask her if she would go with me to the junior prom. When I finally did, she said she already had a date. And with my best friend, Stewart, too. I finally got a date, someone my sister knew, but spent most of the evening watching Stewart's date.

Though we're apart
You're part of me still
For you were my thrill
On Blueberry Hill

I didn't see her during the summer. Not once. I went to the beach almost every day looking for her, but later found out she spent the whole summer with her family in Cape Cod. All I had to show for my efforts by the time our senior year started was a very nice tan.

The wind in the willow played
Love's sweet melody
But all of those vows you made
Were never to be

I looked at her next to me. She finally agreed to go out with me. Probably because Stewart had moved back to Canada with his parents.

Another airplane was landing. We could see it touching down. The moon was low on the horizon and Fats was finishing his song. Now it was time to move in. I put my hand around her shoulder and gently pulled her towards me. She closed her eyes. Our lips touched. She moaned, she was in a dream state, and then she said it.

"Stewart, oh, I've missed you so, so much."

I turned the key, the car started. The moon was gone for the evening. I drove her home. Neither spoke. Not one word. I never saw her again. Last I heard she was in Canada, but I still remember that night on Mount Soledad. And Fats, and that song.

AND THEN THERE WAS THE SUMMER OF '45

HER NAME WAS JOANNE, BUT I didn't know that until later. Much later.

It was the night of the big high school football game. Last game of the season against our cross-town rivals.

I was a senior, and although I wanted to play football, my mom was against it.

"It'll ruin that pretty boy face," she exclaimed, overriding my dad's position that I could play. And since mom's wishes always held, I didn't go out for the team. I just watched from the hard steel bleachers.

Tonight's home game against Jefferson Davis High School was a rout. The Jefferson Davis Rebels were crushing us 45 to 6, and it was only midway through the third quarter.

I decided I had had enough, and so I worked my way down and behind the bleachers on my way to the exit.

It was dark behind the bleachers, but there was just enough light from the stadium lights to make my way. I was alone, until …

I wasn't.

She came out of the darkness in my direction. As she got closer, I could tell by the color of her sweater that she attended Jefferson Davis High.

She stopped directly in front of me. Intentionally I thought, blocking my path to the exit.

She was my height.

I tried to look away, but my eyes kept returning to her bright blue eyes, and to her smile, that mysterious smile.

I wanted to say something, like "excuse me," but couldn't get the words out. I was speechless. Was it her eyes, her smile, her long blonde hair, why couldn't I say anything?

The students in the section directly above us started cheering. Then they began jumping up and down on the steel bleachers.

Suddenly her hands cupped the back of my neck and gently pulled me towards her, closer than I had ever been to a girl. At first, I resisted, but then I gave in.

The noise above us grew louder. The rhythmic banging on the metal bleachers hammered in my ears. It was deafening.

Our lips met.

The cheering intensified. Our student section, which had been silent through most of the game, was suddenly going wild. Something was happening.

Her lips were so smooth and slightly damp. It was my first kiss, other than my mother and my grandmother. But this was different, so different.

The noise above grew even louder. It was like thunder.

Her lips slowly parted, and her tongue rolled against my dry lips. Her hands were in my hair, her fingers massaging my natural curls.

Suddenly there was the booming sound of guns, rifles. Our team had scored, and the usual sound of gun shots followed. Blanks of course. A tradition at Robert E. Lee High School.

As the echoes of the gun fire bounced through the stadium, she gently bit my upper lip.

The taste of blood filled my mouth.

I started to say something as she backed away, but before I could speak, she put a finger to my lips and shook her head, no.

A wild cheer went up as the team returned to the sidelines. The pounding on the steel bleachers continued.

She removed her finger from my bleeding lip and held it in front of me revealing a small drop of blood on her fingertip.

The stadium grew silent as the teams lined up for the kickoff. The only sound I heard was my heavy breathing.

She smiled, and without saying a word, she put her finger to her lips and wiped the blood away with her tongue. And then she brushed past me and into the darkness, out of my life.

The months dragged by, but all I could think about was that encounter under the bleachers. Who and why? And would I ever see her again?

It was an afternoon basketball game at Jefferson Davis High School. I spent most of the game looking at the student section on the other side of the gym. Looking for her. Looking for those blue eyes, that smile and the long blonde hair.

If she was there, I didn't see her.

As I headed to the concession stand for a soft drink I was beginning to wonder if I would ever see her again. I also wondered if that night was just a dream. Was it real, or did I imagine it, imagine that kiss and the taste of blood?

The line was moving slowly, when suddenly I felt someone behind me tapping on my shoulder.

I slowly turned, expecting it was one of my friends wanting to cut in line.

But it wasn't.

It was her.

"Hello," she said.

I just stood there, completely caught off guard. Fumbling for words. Any words.

"Hello," she repeated.

"Ahh," was all I could say.

"Remember me?" She was smiling.

Clearing my throat, I wanted to act cool. But I was far from it. My palms were clammy, but my mouth was as dry as sandpaper. I struggled, but finally I was able to speak. Kind of.

"Oh ... of ... of course... I do... remember you. Yes... I do."

She broke into a soft laugh.

She's making fun of me, I thought.

"I'm JoAnne," she offered.

"Alan."

"Nice to meet you, Alan."

And so we formally met. At last. JoAnne and me.

But we didn't see one another again until the summer.

I was in the city park, fishing in the lake, when I heard a voice behind me.

"Any luck, Alan?"

I turned, and when I saw her, I dropped my fishing pole.

"JoAnne, it's you,"

And so, from that early June afternoon on, JoAnne and I would spend almost every day together at the park. On a few occasions I would bring my fishing pole, but most of the time it was a Coke for me and a Hires root beer for her.

We would sit by the water's edge and talk, sometimes past our dinner times. Sometimes into the early darkness. We could talk for hours.

"So, JoAnne, what do you want to do? What would you like to do?"

"A doctor," she said. "I want to be a doctor, or a nurse. I want to help people and take care of them."

When I told her that would be a wonderful profession, she started crying. And although she didn't tell me at the time, she later told me that her mother suffered from a crippling illness. Polio. And that's why she wanted to help people.

Sometimes when we sat in the cool grass and there was a moment of silence, I would reach over and hold her hand. She never pulled back, but gently squeezed my hand in return.

"And you, Alan, what would you like to do?"

I pointed up to the sky.

"I ... I want to be an airplane pilot."

I expected her to laugh, but instead she replied, "Oh Alan, I could see you doing that. A pilot of one of those big airplanes. And you'd look so handsome in that uniform."

I blushed, and then I thought of my mom. "Pretty boy face." Then I laughed.

"And you could be my co-pilot."

Sometimes we'd talk about the war.

"My dad told me that now that Germany has surrendered, it won't be long before Japan does." It was JoAnne. "Then we can get our lives back to normal. Won't that be nice."

"Yeah," I said, not really knowing what was normal for me, or my parents.

As the weeks went by, I felt my feelings for JoAnne getting stronger. I also realized our kiss under the bleachers, was our only kiss. So, one early evening I decided it was time I made my move.

JoAnne was sitting close to me. Closer than normal. Perhaps it was the chill in the early autumn air, or perhaps it was something else. It was dusk and we were alone. A perfect time, I thought.

I leaned over and gently kissed her cheek. She turned to me, and we kissed as we did under the bleachers. Long and passionate. This time JoAnne just nibbled at my lip. No blood. I was on the top of the world.

I was breathing hard now. She was too.

I reached for the upper button on her blouse. As I started to twist the button, her hand grabbed mine. She pushed me away.

"No, not now, Alan."

"But I thought."

"No, you have to wait."

"Wait?"

"Yes, wait until we're married."

"Married?"

"Yes, married."

Suddenly JoAnne was talking of getting married. And while I knew I liked her, enjoyed her company, I hadn't once thought of marriage.

"Well, you do love me, Alan, don't you?"

As I looked into her blue eyes, and brushed her blonde hair, she repeated,

"Don't you, Alan? Love me."

I didn't know what to say. I didn't know how to respond. I just sat there, looking at her.

For the next week, JoAnne missed our daily meetings at the lake. Not knowing where she lived there was no way I could contact her to see if she was okay.

By the end of the week, I was in a panic. She was mad at me, I thought. She's grown tired of me. How could I think anyone like her could like someone like me?

As soon as I was convinced I would never see her again, she reappeared.

"Are you okay, JoAnne?"

"Yeah."

"I've missed you."

"Oh?"

"Here's a root beer."

She held her hand up to indicate she didn't want one. That's when I noticed she had been crying.

"JoAnne, what's the matter?"

Her hands were cradling her head. Her shoulders were shaking. She started sobbing.

"It's… it's… my mom."

"What? What's happened to your mom?"

Her crying grew louder. Her hands fell to her sides.

"She … she … she."

"What, JoAnne, what?"

"Died."

"But how?"

"Her … illness. The … polio."

Again, I didn't know what to say. I sat down and she lowered herself next to me.

"Just hold me," she said. "Just hold me. Please."

And for the next week, that's all I did. We didn't talk, we didn't kiss. I just held her.

When at the end of the long week, we finally talked, the first thing I said was,

"Yes, yes, I love you. JoAnne, I love you."

She was holding my hands. She was smiling.

"Then we must run away. Leave this place. Go someplace where nobody knows us. Get married."

"But your father, my parents, what are we going to tell them?"

"Nothing, we'll just go."

"I'm not sure…"

"I can't stay here. It's too painful."

"Oh."

"If you don't want to go, I will leave by myself."

Suddenly the thought of JoAnne leaving struck me. I couldn't let that happen.

"Okay, we'll leave together."

"Tonight."

"Tonight?"

"Yes, I'm leaving tonight."

"But how?"

She held up the keys to her dad's car. A new car, an Oldsmobile 98.

"Just meet me here at 10:00. I'll have the car."

She kissed me on the lips and then she jumped up and ran across the freshly cut grass to the parking lot and beyond. Soon she was out of sight, but I could still feel the kiss on my lips. Yes, I was in love.

I slowly rose and started walking home. It was dark now.

Dinner was already on the table.

"Alan, did you forget the time?"

"Sorry mom."

"Where were you at this hour?"

"Just hanging."

"Who you hanging with at this hour?"

"Just some friends, some guys."

"Well, you better not be late again. The next time there'll be no dinner for you, pretty boy."

"Yes mom."

It was 9:30 when I slowly opened my bedroom window. With a

few items stuffed in a pillowcase, I lowered myself to the ground, and dashed across the lawn.

The walk to the park normally took me 15 minutes, but I ran all the way. I was there in five.

Exhausted, I collapsed on the grass next to the empty parking lot.

Looking up at the bright stars I thought about our future.

I had never been up north but heard rumors about the better jobs up there. Better living conditions too.

I thought about my parents. I would miss them, but I would write them and ask them to visit.

But most of my thoughts were about JoAnne.

I was getting tired now and the stars were fading in and out.

Suddenly she was on top of me. Holding me tight. Even in the darkness, I saw her smile.

Then she started pulling at my shirt. It quickly slid over my head. The cold grass tickled my back.

She started to remove her sweatshirt. The Jefferson Davis High imprint disappeared over her forehead.

I reached up and grabbed her hands.

"I thought you wanted to wait."

"What?"

"Wait, we should wait."

"What are you taking about?"

I opened my eyes, I had been dreaming. I sat up.

JoAnne was standing there, looking down at me.

"What are you saying? Are you changing your mind about going with me?"

"Oh no, I was just dreaming. I must have fallen asleep."

"So, are you ready?" She was holding the car keys.

"Yes."

Tossing me the keys, she replied, "well you can drive first."

There was only one highway going north, leaving Mississippi. It would take about three hours to cross into Tennessee.

"Where we headed?" I asked JoAnne.

"Chicago. I have friends in Chicago. They will help us."

"What about your dad? Did he suspect anything?"

"Couldn't tell. He had been drinking when I snuck out."

It was a two-lane road. U.S. highway 45 going north. While there was little traffic this time of night, the lights of the occasional oncoming truck were bothersome. Of course, this was only the third time I had driven a car, but I wasn't about to tell JoAnne.

We entered the northern part of the state. Through the Woodall Mountain range. The road climbed in elevation and curved though the passes.

The road leveled off now, the state line was just a few miles away.

JoAnne woke. She had been sleeping for the last hour.

"How's it going, Alan?"

"Almost in Tennessee."

As she leaned over to kiss me on the cheek, I saw the lights ahead.

"What's that?"

"Not sure, perhaps an accident."

The closer we got, we realized it was not an accident. Two police cars were actually blocking the road.

"What are we going to do?" JoAnne asked in a voice choked with panic.

"Maybe they're looking for some escaped convicts."

"Yeah, that's probably it."

Easing up on the accelerator, I gently pumped the breaks. The Oldsmobile came to a slow stop.

Off to the side of the road was a helicopter. It's blades slowly turning.

There were at least 6 of them. All with their guns drawn.

One of them opened the passenger door and grabbed JoAnne by her arm.

He turned back to the others and shouted, "it's her," and then he turned back to JoAnne.

"Come with me Miss."

Although she resisted, he overpowered her and dragged her out of the car. Then he slammed the car door shut.

I started to open my door when another officer approached.

"And just where in hell do you think you're going?"

"To JoAnne, to my girlfriend."

As he looked at me, I could see the hate in his eyes. A hate I had seen once before. Once when I got on the city bus with my dad, and I sat in the front. The bus driver turned to my dad and pointed to the back. His eyes were full of hate. Just like the policeman standing by the open car door.

"I don't think so. You're not going anywhere."

"Please."

"In case you didn't know it, we don't appreciate you black boys mingling with our white girls."

"But … we're in …"

"Shut your fucking mouth boy."

Suddenly the car started shaking, and the noise was like thumping on metal.

I thought of that night, that night under the stadium bleachers. The sound of those metal bleachers.

And there she was, not under the bleachers, but in front of the car, her fists pounding on the hood.

She was screaming, for me.

Just like the cheering the night we first met.

I looked in her eyes, her smile was gone. She was crying as they pulled her away from the car.

And then that sound, I was back at Robert E. Lee High. We scored a touchdown.

The windshield shattered.

Once again, I could taste the blood in my mouth.

It was like our first kiss. But it wasn't.

PROSECCO, THE WINE OF ITALY

THE AIRPLANES CIRCLED ABOVE. PERHAPS four, five, six of them. It was hard to tell how many as they darted in and out of the dark clouds.

It was the early afternoon. The vineyard was still damp from the morning rain.

The thick cigar smoke slowly drifted up, swirling in the slight breeze. One of many bad habits I had acquired from my father. But I loved the sweet smell. The rich aroma. The coughing, not so much.

The Prosecco, too. Another habit, a good one perhaps, thanks to my father and his father.

Holding the full wine glass up to the sky, I was drawn to the content's golden straw color. A color like the wheat in the fields at harvest time. The lively bubbles reminded me of better times in Italy. I wondered if we'd ever see them again. And I wondered about the Prosecco, the clean and simple fruity flavored Prosecco.

"That'll kill you," he said pointing at the rising cigar smoke. He was 10. My grandson.

"Well, something eventually will," I replied.

"But, Grandpa …"

"No buts, Paolo. And while you're up go get me another bottle of Prosecco. And make sure it's cold, really cold, this time."

Paolo's father was not here. He was up north, near the Brenner Pass. Trying not to be killed.

The Brenner Pass, a pass through the Alps connecting Italy and Austria. One of the most significant routes tying Italy to its neighbors to the north.

The Brenner Pass, where in March 1940, Adolf Hitler met with Benito Mussolini and asked the Italian dictator to ally with Germany's war effort. The "Duce," the political leader of the National Fascist Party of Italy, agreed. On that day, Italy's fate was sealed. Our future was locked with the leader of the "Master Race."

I told him not to go. But he was stubborn, like me.

"I have to, dad."

His mother too asked him not to go. Our only son. Begged him not to go.

"Giuseppe," please don't go. Think of your wife and son. They need you."

"Italy needs me more," was his short reply to his tearful mother.

And that was it. His mind was made up. He left, his son and wife behind. Both of them, with us in the small village of San Pietro di Barbozza, in the Prosecco region of northeast Italy.

San Pietro di Barbozza, in the Veneto, where the climate and rich soil were responsible for producing the best Prosecco in all of Italy, in all of the world.

San Pietro di Barbozza, with its steep hills covered with rows of hanging grape vines. At least before the war. Now it was just random patches of white grapes. Struggling to survive. Like all of us, everywhere. Struggling to survive the horrors of this long war.

By July 1943, with the tide of war turning against Italy, Mussolini again met with Hitler. This time in the northern Italian town of Feltre, located in the Prosecco province of Belluno, where the Prosecco vineyards grow, close to the Alps and the cool breezes that caressed the grapes, produce freshness, and aromas of great finesse.

In Feltre, Mussolini requested additional military assistance from Germany. Hitler agreed to provide it, but only on the condition that Italy be placed under German authority. Mussolini agreed, and on that summer day, our country fell under the complete control of Germany, and der Führer.

I poured myself another Prosecco. The small bubbles rose to the surface. A floral aroma followed. I thought of better times here among the white Glera grapes of San Pietro di Barbozza. Much better times.

Growing up among the grapes of San Pietro di Barbozza, it was only natural that I fell under the spell of the Prosecco. I joined the profession of my father and his father, and assumed my son, Giuseppe, would do the same. It was hard work, but the pull of the grapes prevailed.

But during the war, tending to the grapes had become difficult. Protecting the grapes more so.

After Italy fell under German control, Germany began treating Italy as an occupied nation and the Italians as a subservient people. Hitler also set up a command post in the city of Trieste, a port city in the far northeast corner of Italy.

Trieste. The region where Prosecco was born.

The wine traces its origins back to the 16th century to a city with the same name. Eventually the vineyards moved west from the Trieste region to the richer soil of Veneto, including my village of San Pietro di Barbozza.

I lit another cigar and as I did, I could hear my dad's voice.

"Prosecco and a good cigar, that's all a man needed."

Taking exception, my mom would slap him with a dish towel. Then with both laughing, he would add, "and, of course, a woman who's a good cook."

The airplanes were descending now, looking for a place to land. Perhaps in the valley below San Pietro di Barbozza.

Within a short period of time after the Germans occupied Italy, the Italians turned against them. After disposing of Mussolini, the new Italian government actually declared war on Germany.

Their hatred towards the Germans and their Fascist ideology drove the Italians to form their anti-fascist Comitato di Liberazione Nazionale, the Italian resistance group whose goal was to fight the occupying forces of Nazi Germany.

The dark clouds slowly parted. The rays of the sun reached to the valley below, like giant fingers from the sky to the earth.

"The Conversion of Saul," my wife said. "It reminds me of Michelangelo's painting."

"Huh?"

"The Biblical scene of the transformation of Saul of Tarsus into Paul the Apostle. The golden light of God striking Saul, thus converting him from a cruel persecutor of Christians into one of its foremost advocates."

I almost forgot that my wife was a lover of art, especially Michelangelo di Lodovico Buonarroti.

"Too bad he didn't use it on Mussolini, or Hitler," was all I could think of as a reply.

The planes had landed on a flat open field. Troops were disembarking.

"Another Prosecco?"

"Grazia."

There were three of us now. Three of us sipping the sweet, cool Prosecco. Paolo was looking at the airplanes. I looked at my Prosecco and thought of Ancient Rome.

Writings from the 16th century, describe that the pressing of these Glera grapes produced one of Italy's most sought-after wines. The wine was treasured by the Romans as a true delicacy for its fruity and fresh taste, and with magical qualities that contributed to a long life.

A group of the soldiers were moving up the slopes to San Pietro di Barbozza. There must have been 10 of them. Each carrying a weapon.

"What should we do?" It was my wife.

"Nothing we can do." I replied, sipping the Prosecco.

"Perhaps it's time for another cigar?"

The soldiers had reached the vineyards. Some stopped to taste the grapes.

"Probably bitter," I said.

"What?"

"The grapes. Not even close to ripe."

My grandson was standing next to me. He was holding tightly on to my arm. I could tell he was frightened.

"Grandpa, what's happening?"

"It's okay Paolo."

"But these soldiers. What do they want?"

Before I could answer, the soldiers exited the row of grapes and entered our yard. They were walking towards us. Their rifles were at their sides.

I stood up and with a wave acknowledged and welcomed them to our property.

"Are you okay?" the one in charge asked.

"Yes, we are," I replied.

"We're just checking to see if anyone needs help."

I glanced at his dirty uniform. It was worn and torn in places. The original color was probably faded by the sun. What remained was a light olive-green uniform.

Light olive-green, the color of a cheap Prosecco, I thought. The war had caused shortages, so some vineyards reduced the amount of white Glera grapes. The resulting wine took on a light green color and of course the taste was not even close to a true Prosecco.

We didn't. Our wine was still 100% Prosecco.

"We are fine. But do you have any news on the war?"

The soldier looked at me and a big grin appeared on his face. It was a combination of happiness and relief.

"The Germans have surrendered. Tomorrow, May 7th, they will sign an unconditional surrender at Reims. The war in Europe is over."

I slowly eased myself back into my chair. My eyes were suddenly filled with tears. The words I had been waiting to hear for over 5 years echoed in my head. The war is over. The war is over.

"Giuseppe," my wife uttered. "Our son, we need our son."

The soldier looked at me. He was confused.

"Our son joined Comitato di Liberazione Nazionale and went to Brenner Pass to fight the Nazis," I added.

"I'm sure he'll be home soon," the soldier replied.

"I hope so, at least for harvest time."

"Harvest time?"

"Yes, the Glera grapes, for Prosecco wine."

"Never had it."

"Never?"

"Nope."

I turned to Paolo and thrust my arms upward indicating I don't believe what I just heard.

Paolo smiled. My wife broke out in laughter.

"Paolo," I said, "get ten glasses and a few bottles of Prosecco for these American soldiers. And make sure it's cold."

ARMANDO AND ME

"**D**on't come any closer, or I'll shoot." He was standing against the wall, a Glock 19 in his hand. A half-consumed bottle of Jim Beam at his feet.

"Jesus, Armando, is that you?"

I hadn't seen him for years, too many to remember. But here we were again in this familiar empty factory.

"Huh?"

"Armando, what's the matter?"

"Everything's the matter. Everything's fucked up." He was about to cry. I could sense that in his voice.

"Please, Armando, put down the gun."

"Fuck no, fuck no." He was screaming now. The gun pressed tightly against his temple.

"Armando, calm down."

"Shit, I've never been calmer. I've had enough of this. Now, I know what I gotta do."

"Let's talk, Armando. Can we do that?"

He was once my best friend. We had known each other since grade school. Although Armando was almost a year older, we became best buddies. I didn't realize why at the time, but later it was painfully obvious to both of us.

"There's nothing to talk about. I'm done with all this shit. Done.

Nothing to live for." As he spoke, he gently slid from a standing position to a sitting position. His back resting against the dirty wall. Gun still against his temple.

"But what about your family? Your wife and son. What about them."

"They'll be better off without me. Never did anything for them in the first place. Just trouble."

In high school we hung out with one another. Had to. No one else would let us in. Damn little cliques. No place for us, for our kind. But we had one another.

"How can you say that, Armando? That they'll be better off without you?"

"It's true. They will be."

"So, Armando, were you better off without a dad?"

He didn't say anything. He was looking at me with those big sad eyes. I hit a deep emotional spot with him. It always did.

"So, were you, Armando? Better off after your ..."

"That was different. He didn't leave."

"But you grew up without him."

"Yes, fuck, yes. Because some cop shot him. Killed him. Fuck."

He was looking at my badge. LA police department. But he knew that's what I wanted to do. I didn't need to explain or apologize. I started to move towards him.

"He said, don't come any closer. Do you want me to shoot you too?"

"Oh, Armando, you wouldn't do that. Your brother?"

We were like brothers, even in high school. And after his dad died, our bond grew even stronger, closer. He needed me even more after that. But I needed him too. Perhaps I should have told him that. Now I wish I had.

"No, no. I don't want to, but don't come any closer. Please."

"Armando, talk to me."

"Nothin. There's nothin to talk about. It's settled."

"Settled? What's settled?"

"What I gotta do."

"Armando. Remember in high school. We said we'd be brothers, brothers forever?"

"Yea."

"Brothers don't do this. Brothers don't leave their brothers, not like this."

"What do you know about it? What the hell do you know, Maurice?"

He said it. Maurice, my name. He only used that name when he was angry.

Maurice. All those kids in school made fun of me because of it. Maurice. Maurice. I could still hear them now.

I asked my mom, why? Why, Maurice?

"Dark skin," she answered. It means dark skin, just like yours. Beautiful dark black skin."

I only asked her once, but I never told Armando what she said.

"Armando, did you ever wonder why we became such good friends?"

As he reached for the bottle of Jim Beam, he shook his head from side to side.

"We didn't have a choice, Maurice. Fucking white kids."

"Yeah, we were so different from all those rich white kids."

He pressed the bottle to his mouth. And took a long swig.

"I hated them; I hated my life then. The damn bullying and that wasn't even the worst of it. Shit. Everything was fucked up. Everything."

"Tell me about it, Armando! We were so poor compared to them. Jesus, I wore the same God damn tennis shoes for years, even after the sides split open. Then, in high school I wore my dad's. Of course, he didn't need them where he was."

"Shit, Maurice. Do you ever see him? Your dad?

By the tone of his voice, I could tell he was no longer angry, at least with me. He sounded sympathetic.

"At first, almost every month, but then after my mom met Trevon, we stopped visiting him. We stopped going to the prison. Trevon said it wasn't good to go there, especially for a kid. That we had to move on."

"But now, do you go now?"

"I went a couple of times, but he didn't recognize me. Dementia, I think."

"Jesus, I'm sorry, I didn't know."

"No reason why you should, No reason."

Armando and I had lost contact with one another shortly after high school. I went to the local community college, and he started his own business. Tattoos. Armando's Tattoos. But then he got into dealing and I didn't see him again until now, twenty some odd years later.

"So how come you're here, Maurice? In this crappy part of town?"

"It's my beat. I just happened to be driving by when I got the call on my radio."

"Call?"

"Yeah, someone reported a guy with a gun breaking into this building."

"This building. Maurice, do you remember this building?"

"Of course, I do, Armando. Jesus, how could I forget."

It was an old, abandoned factory. Even back then, it was all closed up, boarded up. Company moved offshore to China. Stripped it of all the equipment and just left. And it's still here today, with a faded for sale sign on it.

"We would come here after school. To our secret meeting place. To sneak a smoke and have a beer."

"Actually, we would run here, to avoid those after school beatings."

Armando started laughing. He put the gun down on the floor next to him.

"Those were the days, Maurice."

"Wouldn't trade them for anything."

"But since then, shit, it's all downhill, at least for me. Run-ins with the law. Jail time too, for dealing."

"Sorry to hear that."

"And what about you, Maurice? Happy? Happy with your life?"

I didn't know how to answer, or even if I wanted to answer, but I think he could see it in my eyes, all the things I couldn't talk about. At least not yet.

"Yeah, I thought so," he said as he offered me the bottle of Jim Beam.

"Armando, remember at graduation we said we wanted to take a road trip together to Vegas."

"Just a dream, Maurice, it was just a dream."

"Well, what are you doing this weekend. It's only 4 hours from LA."

"But my wife and kid."

"Explain it to them, they'll understand. Two old brothers getting together after all these years."

"Maurice, did you ever feel life was not fair?"

"Yes, always actually, I did until today."

"What?"

"Today, now, I realized how life turned us into brothers and without that I would have never made it. We survived because we had each other. I survived because of you, Armando.

Armando stood up and handed me his gun. We hugged in silence for a long time.

"A beer, brother? he said.

"What?"

"How about a beer?"

"Why sure, I'm off in about two hours. Where shall I meet you?"

Armando looked around the empty room and smiled.

"How about here? Our secret hiding place?"

"Sounds good to me. I'll bring the six pack, brother."

"I'll bring the cigarettes."

THE ELEPHANT

IT WAS EARLY MORNING. THE soft light brightened the bungalow.

It was our second day at the Lions Sand Safari Reserve in South Africa.

My eyes were heavy as they attempted to focus on the mosquito net above me. So heavy.

In the far distance, beyond the river, the sounds of elephants broke the morning silence.

"Are you hungry?" I mumbled.

"Perhaps a coffee would be enough," she said.

It was Charmaine.

It had been a long night, the first of our evening safaris.

"Yes, coffee sounds good."

The sound of the elephants grew closer.

"Sounds like they're moving toward the river."

Regrettably, I didn't see any elephants last night. Perhaps they're daytime creatures, I thought. Did see plenty of zebras, their stripes glowing in the floodlight of the Range Rover.

"What time is the morning safari?"

"I think we're meeting in about 60 minutes."

Sipping the dark African coffee, I wondered what animals we'd see this morning. Lions, leopards, elephants, giraffes. Oh, I'd like to see some elephants. They're my favorite.

Outside, the sound of the elephants grew louder. Much louder.

"I wonder if they're heading to the reserve?"

"I'm sure the staff will let us know?"

It had been a week since we had docked in Cape Town. A city with such depressing discrepancies, from the townships to the high-rise condos. From unbelievable poverty to the old rich. After a week, we were ready to leave. More than ready. And of course, a chance to see an elephant.

The ring of the telephone broke my thoughts of Cape Town.

"Hello," she said. "Yes, we will."

"What's that all about?"

"A herd of elephants has broken the barrier surrounding the reserve. The staff wants us to stay in our bungalow."

"Another coffee then?"

"Sure, but two sugars this time. That coffee is ..."

The sound of gun shots stopped me mid-sentence.

"What the hell is that?

"Perhaps the staff is trying to ..."

Just then, more gun shots followed by frantic shouting.

"I'm scared, really scared. What should we do?"

"Stay put," I said. "We're safe in here."

"How do you know that?"

"I would think ..."

A stray bullet crashed through the front window. The sounds of fleeing footsteps outside. More shouting. More gun shots. The cries of elephants. Engines starting. Then the sound of Range Rovers leaving the reserve.

"Christ, is the staff leaving?"

"I think they're gone."

"What's that?"

The elephant crashed through the front of the bungalow. He rose up on his hind legs and waved his long trunk in my direction. The sound was deafening. His eyes met mine. Suddenly I was at peace.

Well, I thought, if I'm going to get crushed, at least I'm getting to see an elephant. My favorite.

"Your coffee's ready."

It was Charmaine. She was shaking me.

My eyes opened. The mosquito net finally came into focus.

"I must have fallen back asleep."

"Well, hurry up. Don't you want to see those elephants this morning?"

FLUFFY

AS HE STARTED TELLING HIS story, a thin moist film covered his eyes.

He was holding back the tears.

His words came slowly and deliberately at first.

But they were his words as was the pain which now appeared on his wrinkled face.

Together they told his story of what it was like. Those dreadful days of his lost youth. The hunger, the crying, the beatings. It was all there, all part of him, and I could tell he wanted to tell it, all of it, perhaps hoping if he did, he would be free of those nightmares. Those nightmares which he had carried ever since those days.

He was just a young boy, he thought around 6 or 7, when it began.

At first it was just marching. Marching through the cobblestone streets of their small village.

Flags too, which he didn't understand. But flags which seemed to worry his parents and his grandparents.

"What's going on? What's happening?" He asked his grandfather.

But his grandfather only shook his head.

He was certain he knew, that his grandfather knew, but he didn't want to tell him.

Perhaps he was afraid to tell him.

His parents, too, did not answer his many questions.

He asked his friends in the old houses next to him, but they had no answers for him.

One day, the marchers stopped in front of his home. He was watching from the big window in the living room.

The marchers started shouting. He could see them, but he didn't know what they were saying. He couldn't make out the words.

Suddenly one of them picked up a rock and threw it at the house.

As the rock crashed through the window, pieces of glass scattered throughout the room. A large piece cut into his face.

"Here," he said, pointing to a fading scar on his left cheek. "Here's where the glass embedded into my face."

He gently rubbed the scar as if to remind him of that day. As if to give him courage to continue with his story.

He took a breath, a shallow breath, coughed twice, and continued speaking.

His dad had a shop next to their house.

It was his grandfather's shop, but most of the time his grandfather was too tired, or too ill, to leave the house and go next door. On those occasions he would help his father.

The shop was a bakery.

His dad would bake bread early every morning and when it came out of the ovens, his dad would open the front door to announce his bread was ready.

A smile came over his face as he remembered that moment. His favorite moment of the day. The smell of freshly baked bread filling the neighborhood. Calling buyers to his father's bakery.

Soon posters appeared. Plastered to shops around the village.

They were movie posters. A poster of an evil looking man with the movie title, Jew Süss.

He asked his grandfather what the movie was about, but he refused to tell him.

Years later he would learn about the 1940 German propaganda film, Jew Süss, which was regarded as one of the most anti-Semitic films of all time.

One morning the poster appeared on the door of his dad's bakery.

His dad wanted to pull it off, but his father advised him not to.

"Don't arouse suspicion," his father told him. "Better to remain unnoticed."

But then that poster appeared on their front door.

His dad couldn't take that, and he tore it down. Ripped it up and threw it into the street.

That was the beginning. The beginning of the terror against his family.

More rocks smashed through their windows. And a strange symbol was painted on their front door. It was a hooked cross. It was the first time he had seen something like that.

But it wouldn't be the last time.

His mother tried to wash off the symbol, and when she did, it would reappear the next morning.

Waving me closer, he continued with his story.

One morning he woke up to the smell of a fire. Smoke was drifting into his small upstairs bedroom through an open crack in a window.

Outside, people were cheering.

He rushed downstairs and out the front door.

His parents and grandparents were there. Just standing there.

Suddenlt, he felt the heat from the fire.

He turned to his father's bakery and realized where the smoke was coming from.

The flames had engulfed the entire shop. The remaining windows were popping from the searing heat. The old wood was snapping and cracking. Sparks were drifting upwards, carried along with the spiraling smoke.

A crowd of young boys in brown uniforms was wildly cheering on the fire.

Suddenly they broke into chant,

"Ein Volk, ein Reich, ein Führer."

He quickly translated the words into the English his mother was teaching him.

"One People, One Country, One Leader." Over and over, they repeated their chant. Louder and louder.

Then he noticed the flags they were waving.

Large flags with a red background, a white disk and a crooked cross in the middle. The same hooked cross which kept appearing on their front door.

He turned to his grandparents. His grandmother was sobbing. She had buried her head in his grandfather's chest, and he was holding her. His hands were shaking.

His mother had collapsed, and his father was helping her to her feet. They were both crying.

He wanted to scream, and he did.

"Why? Why are you doing this?"

One of the boys in the brown uniform walked over to him. He was smiling, but it wasn't a friendly smile.

He asked again, "why are you doing this?"

The punch was swift and hard. He fell backwards onto the hard sidewalk.

More boys in brown uniforms approached. They were standing over him. One spit, and others followed. He tried to turn away. His face was covered.

"Why?" Again. "Why?"

His tears were mixing with their spit. He tried to wipe his face clean. It was no use. He was embarrassed. He wanted to run. Hide.

As if on cue, the boys, all of them, raised their right hand. Their stiff arms and fingers extending to the sky.

And then he heard it for the first time,

"Sieg Heil, Sieg Heil."

But it wouldn't be the last time he would hear it. As with the flag with the hooked cross and the strange salute, he would hear and see them many times in the months ahead. And every time he did, they would strike a terrible fear in him.

But, of course, he didn't know that then. That it was their intended purpose. Fear. Terrible fear.

For the rest of the day the bakery smoldered. After the boys in the brown uniforms left, some neighbors tried to help his dad in putting out the fire.

But it was too late.

The bakery was gone. All that remained were the melted metal ovens.

Their grotesque shapes now just a reminder of the past, the bread, and the smells.

And, as he would later realize, an omen of the future.

A week later, there was a loud knock at their door.

It was dark outside and at first no one wanted to answer.

But the knocking persisted. Louder and louder causing the remaining unbroken windows in their home to rattle.

So, his dad carefully opened the door.

An official looking man stood in the doorway. He was wearing a police uniform. On the right arm of his black jacket, just below the shoulder, there was a red band, with a white circle and the crooked cross. A large German shepherd sat at his side.

The man didn't say hello, but instead he handed something to his dad.

Then he spoke,

"You are to display these badges every time you leave your house. Each of you. Attach them to your shirts, upper right side. Failure to do so will result in immediate arrest."

And that was all.

He turned and with his large dog, he made his way to the next house.

His mother sewed the badges on to their shirts. Her hands trembled as she did because she knew they had to be perfect.

Perfect. The six-pointed yellow star. Placed on the right side like they were instructed. Visible at all times.

The star made out of coarse yellow cloth.

The yellow star, with the word 'Jew' printed in the middle

It needed to be perfect.

He asked his grandfather why they had to wear these. What did they mean?

"The star represents the Star of David," his grandfather told him.

"The star is intended to identify us, to humiliate us and to mark us out for segregation and discrimination."

"But why, grandpa? Why us?" He asked.

"Only because we are Jews, Noah. That's the only reason."

He was confused by his grandfather's explanation. What did he do to them? The boys in the brown uniforms.

And then one day he heard a truck coming down their cobblestone street. It stopped just outside.

A voice was booming through a bullhorn.

"By orders of the national government, all Jews are required to immediately assemble outside. Do not bring any personal belongings or pets."

He was really confused now. Afraid too.

His father opened the front door.

Outside many of their neighbors had gathered on the cobblestone street. No one was speaking.

The man with the bullhorn walked up to them. He was carrying a gun.

"That means you too, get down there on the street. Now."

He and his family started walking down the broken stairs in the direction of the street.

Just then his dog, Fluffy came through the open door and jumped at his feet.

"Fluffy," he said. "What about Fluffy?"

The man with the bullhorn kicked Fluffy away.

"I said no pets."

He wanted to explain to the man that Fluffy went everywhere with him. That Fluffy was his best friend, but before he could say a word, the man with the bullhorn reached for his gun.

He didn't know what was happening, but then his mother put her hands over his eyes.

He heard the shots. Two of them. They echoed off the buildings on the other side of the street.

Even today, when he closes his eyes, he hears the two shots. The two shots and the piercing, whining of Fluffy.

As dad walked him down to the cobblestone street, the man with the bullhorn shouted, "I said no pets."

Dad told him not to look back, but he did. He shouldn't have, but he did. He fell to his knees and started crying.

He cried all the way to the train station. He was still crying when they all boarded the train. All he could do was think of Fluffy. And cry.

The crowded train moved through the night. He was hungry, but there was nothing to eat. He was thirsty, but there was nothing to drink.

He noticed other people were crying and that made him cry even more. His mother brushed his curly hair with her callused hands. But it didn't help. He continued to cry.

In the early daylight hours, the train came to a stop. The hiss of steam woke him.

The train doors opened. They had reached their final destination.

The camp. He was told it was a camp. But it wasn't really a camp.

There were no swings or slides. No playgrounds. No soccer fields.

And there was no leaving. High walls and men with guns saw to that.

And every day, more people arrived. All of them with the Star of David on their shirts.

When they arrived, they were given clothing to wear. It wasn't clean, but it was the same. Striped shirts and striped pants. Their shoes were confiscated. Some were given old slippers.

No, it wasn't a camp. It was hell.

He slept in a broken-down wooden barracks, with a leaky roof. On a tiny wooden bunk bed. Straw-stuffed mattresses, no covers, no pillow.

He had to share his bed with another person. An old man, who coughed throughout the night.

At night he shivered from the cold, and the rain.

No, it wasn't a camp. It was hell.

After the morning roll call, he marched to work.

His job was removing the buttons from the clothing taken from the new arrivals.

At the end of each exhausting day, he fell onto his bunk, dreading the next morning.

No, it wasn't a camp. It was hell.

Breakfast was bread, lunch was soup, and dinner consisted of more bread and occasionally a small piece of meat. The meals were terrible, and never enough.

He was always hungry.

No, it wasn't a camp, it was hell.

One day he noticed that some of the people who had been sleeping in his barracks were gone. Others had taken their place.

His parents and grandparents were in the barracks next to his.

Every morning, before roll call, he would walk to their barracks to be with them.

One morning, strangers were sleeping in their beds.

He asked one of the men with a gun, where his family was, and the man just smiled. He asked again.

"Please, sir, show me where they are."

The man smiled again. A smile like that smile from that boy in the brown uniform when his dad's bakery was on fire. And then the man spoke,

"Don't worry, you'll be joining them shortly."

But the months went by, and he never joined them. And he never asked again where they were.

It was a cold month, snow was on the ground.

Someone said it was January. 1945.

He looked around the camp. All the men with guns were gone. It was very quiet.

He was standing under the gated entrance to the camp, with the others.

The large sign above them spelled out 'Arbeit Macht Frei.'

He first saw that when he entered the camp, so long ago.

"Strange," he thought, "Work Will Set You Free," but of course it didn't. Work did not set anybody free from the camp.

Suddenly he saw them approaching.

Those around him started crying. Some stared in disbelief. Others were too weak to stand.

As the soldiers approached, he wanted to tell his parents and grandparents that everything was going to be okay, that they could come out of hiding.

But they weren't there. They weren't hiding.

It was like they had never been there in the camp. But of course, they had once. In the barracks next to his.

He thought of his dad's bakery. The ovens, the bread, the smell.

He started crying as he remembered hearing rumors of the ovens at the camp.

But they weren't just rumors.

They were real. And they didn't smell like his dad's fresh bread.

He didn't know at the time what the smell was.

But he could close his eyes now and think back. Remember.

When he did, he realized that the smell was the smell of death.

No, it wasn't a camp, it was hell.

As the memories rushed back, he stopped talking. He was crying. Softly.

I reached for his hand.

Then I saw the numbers burned into his arm.

He was finished with his story. The story I had heard many times before. And like the past, I didn't know how to comfort him. How to comfort my father. How to make it better for him. How to push the nightmares away. But this time I would try. I had to.

"Dad, it's alright. I'm here with you."

"Huh."

"You're not in the camp anymore."

He looked at me, with a puzzled expression. Then he spoke, "I miss him."

"Who dad? Who do you miss?"

"Fluffy."

LEWIS AND CLARK, MERI AND ME

THE EARLY MORNING SUN QUICKLY warmed my sleeping bag.

As it did, the temperature rose from warm to uncomfortably hot.

I scrambled out of the old sleeping bag to escape the heat.

"Morning Johnny."

It was Meri. He was in the sleeping bag next to me.

"Morning Meri."

"Got any smokes?"

"Only half a fag."

"Can we share?"

"Always."

Meri and I were friends. I wouldn't say the best of friends, but close enough to share a cigarette.

Our meeting two months ago was unplanned. I was in Billings, Montana. Looking for passage to the northwest. Free passage, of course.

The freight train was headed that way. Its steam engine was smoking, and the wheels were ready to roll.

We both ran for the open boxcar at the same time.

It was dark and we waited until the train was just starting to leave the station before we dashed for the opening. Any earlier and we were sure to be seen. Caught. Didn't want that to happen, cause the last time

I tried to board a train outside of Fargo, I jumped on too early and ended up in jail for almost a week.

It was 1930 and the country was in the midst of something called a depression. Jobs were impossible to find, and in fact many had lost their jobs. Times were tough.

I told my dad I was going to hitchhike to the west coast.

"Might as well do something exciting. Better than just sitting around."

My dad was okay with my planned adventure, but he cautioned that I better not tell mom.

"She'll be really upset, sad too," he warned me. "And don't tell your sisters. They'll only tell mom, then we'll both have a big mess on our hands. I'll tell mom after you leave."

Taking dad's advice, I quietly slipped out of our New York apartment one morning. It was dawn and the streetlights had just turned off. An ice truck and a milk truck were the only vehicles on the street. Early deliveries.

As I left, I passed my dad's barbershop. The shop wasn't opened yet, but he was there getting ready for his customers. Lining up his scissors, combs, clippers, etc.

"A barber will always have work," he bragged, "even when times are bad."

He was right.

And although his regular customers waited longer for a haircut, eventually they showed up. They had to.

"You should consider becoming a barber," he once told me. "You'll always be able to put food on your family's table."

But I wanted something different. Something more exciting. And while I didn't know exactly what that might be, I thought perhaps my journey to the west coast might provide an answer.

The sun just broke through the morning dawn when dad switched on the barber pole. The red, white, and blue bands spiraled upwards announcing that the barbershop was now open for business.

"Bloodletting," my dad told me when I asked about the colors on the pole.

"Back in the Middle Ages, barbers did a lot more than haircuts and shaves. Barbers also offered certain medical services, like bloodletting. The thinking was that too much blood in one area of the body led to illnesses, so removing some of it would make a person better."

I stopped in front of the shop's window hoping he would notice me. He did.

With a smile and a slight wave, he bid me good travels.

I waved back and turned the corner on my way to the west coast.

"Did you know this rail line follows the route of Lewis and Clark?" It was Meri. He handed me the half cigarette after a long drag.

"Huh?"

"Lewis and Clark, 1804 to 06, from St. Louis to Astoria, Oregon."

"Oh that."

"Yeah that. Well, these Northern Pacific tracks trace their journey."

"Okay."

"Didn't you learn that in school?"

"Of course, Lewis and Park."

"Clark."

"Right, Clark."

Of course, I couldn't tell Meri that I dropped out of school. I didn't even tell my parents.

First year of high school and that was it. Couldn't take the bullying. Dago this, Dago that. And then the beat downs. Dago and the beat downs. Nope, I couldn't go back.

So, I spent my high school years looking for odd jobs. Mostly non-union work around the rail yards, loading and unloading cargo off trains. And at night, occasionally delivering illegal booze to hidden speakeasies. It was prohibition, after all.

And, on the day I would have graduated, I told my dad I was leaving the city to go west.

"You know they ate dogs?" It was Meri again.

"Huh?"

"Lewis and Clark."

"Oh."

"Yeah. They traded for them with the Indians when they ran low on food. According to the records they kept, over two hundred. Two hundred dogs."

I reached in my ragged backpack and pulled out a can of sardines. It was the last of my food supply and I knew Meri was out. I held up the dented can of sardines and started to laugh.

"Well, if we don't score some food today, I guess we might be eating dog tomorrow."

"Or perhaps cat. I think I would prefer cat."

After a couple of sardines for breakfast, we rolled up our dirty sleeping bags, and headed for the highway.

The train we hopped on in Billings only went to Garrison, so the journey to Missoula would be on foot, or if we were lucky, we'd hitch a ride.

The road to Missoula was unpaved.

A washboard dirt road.

One farm truck passed us going in the opposite direction, showering us in a large cloud of brown dust.

The sun was directly overhead.

Not a cloud in the sky.

It was hot.

The half can of sardines was clearly not enough.

I was still hungry.

I was miserable.

I threw down my backpack.

"How the hell did they do it?" I shouted in frustration.

"Seven miles a day. That's how they did it."

"Christ, why?"

"The President asked them. Jefferson was hoping there would be a water route to the Pacific which could open up the west."

"And?"

"Of course, there was none, but their journey to explore the lands west of the Mississippi was still a success in that it provided important information about this uncharted area of North America."

"How long did it take them?"

"A year and a half from St. Louis to the Pacific Ocean."

Suddenly we heard a clunking noise behind us. As we turned, we could see a rising cloud of dust.

The old farm truck was returning. It was bouncing over the washboards.

It slowed and then stopped alongside of us.

"You need a ride?"

"Yeah, could sure use one," I replied.

"We'll I'm going as far as Missoula, if that'll help."

"Sure will, thanks."

"You have to ride in the back on the truck. In the cargo bed. My cab is full of tools and clutter."

"That's okay."

We threw our backpacks and sleeping bags into the open cargo bed and pulled ourselves up and over the side rails.

The cargo bed was lined with hay and worse.

"Smell that?" I whispered to Meri.

"Sheep dung." He replied.

"Jesus Christ."

"Well, would you rather walk the 73 miles to Missoula?"

"I guess not."

"As for walking, perhaps you didn't know this, but Lewis and Clark wore moccasins on part of their journey. Shoes had given out, so they were forced to trade for moccasins."

"Jesus, really?"

"Yeah. And the moccasins had to be replaced every few days as they wore out because of the rough terrain."

As I settled against the back of the cab I looked down to my feet. My ragged Keds had served me well. Moccasins, I thought. God, I'm not complaining about my sore feet again.

The 3-hour ride was uneventful. Had to stop twice for some cows that decided to take a nap in the middle of the road. But for the most part we bounced our way into Missoula.

"The trick is to ask for work at a place that can feed you."

That was the advice Meri gave me the first night we met. And it worked. Cleaning dishes at a restaurant was the best. And it was generally less work than chores on a farm.

We managed to find work. Washing dishes at the Old Missoula Diner. After dinner we headed to the train station. The freight yards would be close.

The sun was setting behind the mountain range to the west.

"That's the Bitterroot Mountains," Meri said pointing to the snowcapped mountains.

"We're not hiking up those?" I replied.

"Hell no, not us. But Lewis and Clark did."

Meri just stood there. Not moving, staring at the 9,000-foot peaks.

"It was mid-September. The weather was beginning to change, frost at night and snow on the mountains. It turned out to be the most treacherous part of their entire journey."

He continued to stare at the mountains. His gaze was fixed.

"The Indians told them they could make the journey in six days."

"And?"

"Well, it took them eleven days to complete the 200 miles. Every day they had trouble locating a place to set up camp and finding grass to feed their horses. Supplies ran low, and with the early winter, most of the men suffered from frostbite."

"It must have been miserable."

"Lewis later wrote in his report that it was a cold and hunger which I shall ever remember."

By the time we reached the train station it was almost dark. A dog had followed us most of the way.

"Hey Meri, that dog has taken a liking to you. It's almost as if he knows you."

The large dog suddenly jumped up and rested his big paws against Meri's hips. His tail was wagging, and he was barking. Not an aggressive bark. Just a soft bark, like a greeting.

"Seaman," was all that Meri said.

"What?"

"Lewis took his dog with him on the journey. A Newfoundland waterdog by the name of Seaman."

"His dog."

"Yes, and Seaman completed the entire journey."

"You mean they didn't eat him too?"

"Hell no, he was Lewis' loyal companion. Why would they eat him?"

"Just asking."

"No way, Lewis would let 'em eat his dog. No way."

As we settled in the thick bushes near the freight track, I finally asked Meri a question which had been bothering me for weeks.

"Hey Meri, how come you know so much about Lewis and Clark?"

Meri turned to me and smiled,

"I just find their adventure, the Corps of Discovery, so fascinating. The 41-man crew of volunteers, soldiers and one African American slave. Over 8,000 miles there, and back."

"A slave joined them?"

"Yes, Clark brought one of his slaves. His name was York. And York completed the entire expedition. York was also the first slave to see the Pacific Ocean."

"Clark had a slave?"

"Yeah, a young black man. Born on Clark's estate, in Caroline County, Virginia."

"Jesus. How did the group feel about a slave joining them?"

"Well, at first they weren't too happy about it, but quickly York became a vital member of the expedition. He hunted for food, smoothed relations with Native American tribes, cared for the sick and helped discover new plants and animals. He even helped Clark in preparing maps of the journey. Yes, York was an invaluable member on that journey."

Meri hesitated for a moment, almost like he was embarrassed by what he was about to tell me. He cleared his throat and then continued.

"But after the voyage's conclusion in September 1806 when they were back home and while the others basked in newfound fame, land grants and financial rewards, all York asked for was his freedom for his services. Just his freedom. And ..."

Meri stopped without revealing what happened. I was curious.

"So, what happened to York?"

"And ... and Clark said no. God damn it, Clark wouldn't give this 30-year-old black man his freedom. He just ... refused."

Meri didn't talk after that for the rest of the evening. Even when we settled in the open boxcar headed into northern Idaho and on to Spokane, he remained silent. I could tell he was upset.

The ride from Missoula to Spokane was a little over four hours. It was still dark when we jumped off the slowing train as it pulled into the station.

As we made our way out of the freight area, Meri finally said something,

"All York wanted was his freedom. That's all. Damn you, Clark. God damn you."

Meri never spoke of York again, at least until we reached the Pacific.

After a few days in Spokane, we made our way to the Columbia River. Ahead was the Pacific Ocean.

I could tell that Meri was becoming more excited the closer we got to where Lewis and Clark first saw the Pacific.

Meri's voice grew louder and stronger. I felt he was telling me a story.

"The closer they got to the Pacific, the more they suffered. They were in canoes now, and they had to paddle through pounding rain and crashing waves. Almost everyone got seasick. Even York."

"The final sixteen miles took ten days. Ten miserable days. They thought they would never see the ocean. That they would certainly fail, or that they might die."

"But finally on November 15, 1805, in the mid-morning, they reached the Pacific Ocean, at the mouth of the Columbia River. Exactly one year, six months, and one day after leaving St. Louis, Missouri, they arrived."

Meri paused for a minute, then he continued his story.

"It was a clear morning. A beautiful morning. An early fog had lifted. The sky was a deep blue. Sea gulls circled above. The waves looked like small mountains rolling across the sea, crashing into the jagged rocks."

Finally, Meri and I were standing at the very spot where Lewis and Clark first saw the Pacific Ocean.

"It was here that Lewis and Clark carved their names and the date into the soft stone."

I tried to imagine what it must have been like for them as the cool ocean breeze slapped against my face. What were they thinking? What were they saying?

"It must have been something?" I mumbled to Meri.

"It was. It certainly was."

"Lewis and Clark standing right here. Right here, Meri. I can almost sense what it was like for them."

"I'm so glad you can, Johnny. So glad."

Meri fell to his knees. He was silently praying.

Minutes later he slowly he rose.

"A little prayer, Meri?"

"Yes ... yes, for York."

He stood erect and proud. Like he was standing at attention. His eyes looked straight ahead. He was focused on the ocean. He seemed to be in a trance, and it was like I wasn't even there. Like he wanted to be alone.

I glanced down at the marker which was placed at the very spot where Lewis and Clark stood on that November day, 125 years ago

I started reciting the inscription on the shiny face plate.

"In 1804-06, Captains Meriwether Lewis and William Clark led about 40 soldiers and boatmen on an epic journey..."

Suddenly I stopped reading.

But I silently repeated the words over and over in my head. Captains Meriwether Lewis and William Clark. Meriwether. Meri ... wether. Meri.

I spun around,

"Meri," I shouted, "what's going on? Who are you."

But there was no one there. Meri was gone. He was nowhere to be seen.

I was confused, almost in a panic.

Frantically I ran over to a couple a few yards away. They were staring at me. As I approached, they backed away.

"Excuse me," I pleaded. "Did you see where that guy went? The guy who was standing next to me. I seem to have lost him."

They looked at one another and then back to me. The man spoke slowly, deliberately, as if he was confused too.

"Actually … you were alone."

"No, I wasn't. I was with Meri … Meriwether." I shouted.

"I'm sorry, but there was no one with you, but …"

"What? Please tell me."

"We thought it was kind of odd that you were carrying on a conversation with yourself."

I turned and looked back at the marker, then off to the ocean, then behind me to the Columbia River. I smiled then started laughing.

"I don't think so," I said. "No, I don't think so."

CHICKEN TERIYAKI

THE COFFEE WAS HOT, ACTUALLY, too hot. The tip of my tongue stung. But it was strong and black, just the way I liked it. No damn cream or sugar for me. Drank it this way in the army and intend to do so until the day I die.

Unlike these young kids today. Damn pumpkin lattes, coffee with soy milk, ice vanilla lattes. Jesus Christ, how can you taste the fucking coffee. Should be against the law, I wrote. Letter to the editor of the local newspaper. They never did reply, or print it. They probably drank those damn designer coffees, too.

I am sitting on the big porch, overlooking the beach. The cool breeze from the ocean was kissing my face. After all those years in the big city, it had come to this.

Two young couples walked by on their way to the beach. Teenagers, for sure. The girls were wearing those skimpy bikinis. Too revealing. No modesty. None at all. Why do their parents let them get away with dressing this way? Christ, this generation. What the hell is wrong with them? Next, they'll be going nude to the beaches.

The coffee was the right temperature now. Kind of bitter, but that's okay. That's the way it was in the army. We never complained. Too busy dodging bullets from God damn Japanese rifles. April 1, 1945, Okinawa. Took that bullet the first day we landed. Was proud to serve too. Unlike kids today. Give peace a chance. Jesus, what the fuck is that all about? We went, we didn't complain. It was the right thing to do. For the country. Not like today. Fucking kids.

My arthritis was acting up this morning. That damn Japanese bullet that was still lodged in my back. Too risky to remove it, the doctors said. Think of it as a souvenir of the war, my buddies said. Shit yes, I did, and I didn't complain. Because I was proud to go. Proud of the damn flag. Unlike kids today. Shit, they wear the flag on their clothes, on their butts.

And today it's okay to burn it. Old Glory. Jesus H. Christ. Why would any court say it's okay? Damn Supreme Court, with all those freaking liberal judges. They're destroying this country.

Two Mexican guys walked past the porch. I've seen them before. I don't like them. I don't trust them. They were speaking Spanish. Spanish.

"Hey you two beaners, speak English. This is America. Damn it, speak English."

They stopped and looked at me.

"English, sure. Fuck you, old man. There's your English."

They walked away, raising their hands, giving me the middle finger. I struggled to stand up, but the damn bullet in my back sent a sharp pain down my legs. The coffee from my coffee mug sloshed over, onto my shirt. Jesus Christ, Jesus Christ. I slumped back down in my chair.

Probably illegals, I thought. Ruining the country.

The country's not the same. Not like it was before the war, when I was growing up. It was so nice then, so comfortable. It was just us. Americans. No illegals.

I thought back to the small town, where I grew up, before the war. Everyone knew their place. No one rocked the boat. No trouble then. No protests. No women's libers. No Gay Pride. No Black Lives Matter. No damn gangs, either. Yes, life was simple. My parents kept telling me, this is the real America, here in the south. But no more. Jesus Christ no more.

"More coffee. Would you like another coffee?"

"Just black, no God damn sugar, or cream. And not too hot. Last time it was too damn hot."

"But of course. By the way, would you like a clean shirt."

"Fuck no."

It was Steve, one of the care givers. I didn't much care for him. Too young. What the hell could he possibly know about old people like me. And I didn't like it when he touched me. His hands were too smooth. I told the manager, I wanted a different care giver, but they refused. Deal with it, they said. Jesus, why did I have to deal with it, a Chinese care giver. I wanted somebody like me. Someone who looked like me, talked like me, thought like me. But he's an American, just like you, born in Los Angeles, they said. I didn't believe them. Illegal, I thought. Had to be, with a last name like Chen. Shit yes, he had to be.

It was lunchtime. As usual they would bring me my lunch on a stand-up tray.

Steve set the tray down in front of me.

"What the fuck is this?"

"Chicken teriyaki and rice."

"What?"

"Japanese. Very popular here in the facility."

"Fuck no. Nothing Japanese for me. Take it away. Bring me a hamburger and fries. Something American. And where the hell is my damn coffee?"

He lifted the tray and turned to leave. I heard him mumble something.

"What's that?"

"Nothing sir, just a slight cough."

Sir, that's right. Show me some damn respect. I earned it. And, not just for taking that damn Japanese bullet, but also for my many years on the police department, keeping the streets safe. Safe from ...

My thoughts wandered. Safe from what? Safe for whom?

I remember coming home after the war. Months in the VA hospital. Dealing with that Japanese bullet. That's where I met her, Loretta.

She was a nurse. But she was a lot more than a nurse.

Loretta, the nurse, my nurse, I remember her like it was yesterday. That smile, that laugh, that touch.

"Good morning, Larry. How we today." She would ask, every

morning. Sometimes I would just lie in bed, with my eyes closed, waiting for her, waiting to hear that voice, waiting for her touch. Such a lovely way to start my day, I thought. If only I could start every day like this.

But of course, I couldn't. I was released. I went home. First in a wheelchair, then later with a cane.

"You look so sophisticated with that cane," she said. It was Loretta. We were dating.

"Really?"

"Yes, and so handsome too."

Life was perfect. I had moved into an apartment in the big city. Soon I was walking without a cane and then I became a policeman. Loretta moved in with me. I was so happy. We both were.

"Coffee's ready." It was Loretta. She was bringing me my morning coffee. I was sitting on the balcony overlooking the city. The sun was out. It was warm. It was perfect.

"Thanks honey."

"Here it is, with cream and sugar, just like you like it. Extra hot too." She was smiling. That perfect smile. God, I was so happy. I couldn't imagine a life without her.

"Sit down, I want to ask you something."

She sat and snuggled next to me. I took a sip of the coffee. So sweet, so hot, just the way I like it. Not like that awful coffee in the army.

"What do you want Larry?"

"I've been thinking," I hesitated, fearful of what she might say.

"What Larry, what is it?"

I turned to her and blurted it out.

"Will you marry me?"

She was silent. She looked away.

"Larry, I … I wonder, that would be wonderful, but … you know."

"It'll work out, you'll see, we'll talk to them."

The drive south took two days. We didn't talk much. Just thinking a lot about what was to come. What might happen.

I knocked on the door of the old colonial house. I was holding her hand, as tight as I could. She didn't say anything.

The door opened. It was the maid.

"Why hello, mister Larry. So nice to see you."

We entered. The big sitting room was like it was before I went off to the war. Somethings never change, I thought.

"Please sit down, I'll tell them you're here."

We decided to stand.

After a brief time, they both came into the sitting room.

"Mother, father, I'd like you to meet Loretta."

You could hear a pin drop, Loretta said on the drive back to the city.

"Loretta and I are getting married, and I wanted to tell you both in person."

Another pin dropped. I waited for their response.

"What do you have to say? Do we have your blessings?"

My dad looked at me, then at Loretta.

"Never. Have you lost your senses, Larry?"

"Have you lost your mind," it was my mother's turn, "what will the family say?"

"Who cares, we're in love and I want to marry her." I felt Loretta's hand pull away from me.

They were both angry now, I could see it in their eyes, in their stiff posture, hands folded in front of them.

"But Larry, look at her. How could you? She's Asian."

And there it was, the two words that changed my life forever, "she's Asian." The last two words I would ever hear from them.

As they left the room, I turned to Loretta. She was not crying. She was expressionless.

"I tried to tell you," she said, "that it just wouldn't work."

On the drive back to the city, we didn't speak. I didn't know what to say. We didn't even stop for the night. We just wanted to get away as quickly as possible.

Arriving at my apartment, she got out of the car and said goodbye. I never saw or heard from her again. She was out of my life. Forever.

My back is acting up again. That bullet. I looked out over to the beach to the waves so far away. I suddenly realized that all my hate, all my rage all these years was misplaced. It has nothing to do with everything and everyone around me.

I could trace it back to those two words, "she's Asian." Those two words that changed my life and not for the good.

Steve is back from the kitchen, standing over me with a tray. A hamburger and fries.

He sees the tears running down my cheeks and bends down toward me. I feel his smooth hands on my bare arm.

"Hey, Larry, are you okay?

"Yes, I am now. I'm okay now."

"That's good, Larry, that's good."

"Say Steve …"

"Yeah, what Larry?"

"Could I try that chicken teriyaki?"

COMING OUT

"HOLD ON, WE'RE COMING FOR YOU."

The smoke was creeping under my front door. Even with the wet towel I had placed as a barrier, the smoke was breaking through. I could feel the heat of the fire drawing closer. Like a snake zeroing in on its victim, slithering ever so close. Relentless. And I was on the top floor. Twenty floors up.

"The view from here is to die for," the real estate agent said.

I should have taken her words literally, I thought. I turned to look out the window. Well, even with all the smoke, the view was incredible. The Pacific Ocean, the Golden Gate Bridge, Alcatraz, I could see them all. Even Angel Island.

"Why do you want to move to San Francisco?" my parents asked. I had just finished college, Florida State. Why do you want to leave Florida?"

I couldn't tell them. Someday perhaps, but not then. Yes, someday I would.

My car was packed, I was ready to leave.

"Will you call?" my mom was crying.

"Of course, I will, mom. You know that."

My dad hugged me. He always did. I would miss that. Perhaps that was the most difficult part of leaving, along with my mom's lasagna, of course. I was struggling to hold back my tears.

"Take care of yourself. Be careful," he whispered.

I wondered again. Did he know? Did they suspect? But how could I ask?

"I will dad."

I sat in the car for minutes, holding the keys in my hand. I looked over at their house. They were standing on the porch. Mom was still crying. Dad was holding her. They didn't want me to leave, but I had to. I had to leave.

The engine turned over. I waved, as I slowly pulled away. Pulling away, I thought. Pulling away from my old life to begin my new life.

The smoke was pouring into my entry way now. I walked over to the front door. I put my hand against it. My God, it was so hot. The snake must be right outside, ready to pounce. But it would have to wait. The door was holding.

The highway out of Florida was crowded. Snowbirds, we called them, heading back north. Back to their estates in New England. But they'd be back next winter, just before it was time to shovel the snow. They were like migrating birds. Back and forth.

The farther west I drove, the more liberated I felt. At last, I was starting to feel true to who I was. Who I had really been for a long time. I was shedding that person I hid behind. He was slowly fading away. It felt good.

Through Georgia, Alabama, Mississippi. No way I could settle here. They certainly wouldn't welcome my kind. Not here, in the Deep South. Perhaps decades from now they might. But I didn't have time to wait. I wanted to be true to myself, now.

Texas took forever. Not much to see, but such a long time to see nothing, I thought. Couldn't live here either. No way. Especially after all the stories I had read about Texas. Too conservative. They'd run me out of the state, or worse.

The fire broke through the front door. The snake was looking in. I shut the door to my bedroom. My last holdout, I thought. The snake would be here soon.

I certainly didn't fit into the role expected of me by my family, by my close friends, even many of my fellow students. I felt afraid and isolated. Yes, definitely isolated. That's why I had to leave. That's why I wanted to go to San Francisco. Had to go.

It was my second year in college, when I met Scott. He too felt isolated. "I can hardly wait to get away from here," he would say.

"Where will you go," I asked.

"Anywhere but the south. Perhaps some Nordic country. I hear they're more accepting."

He finished college the year before I did. As he was leaving, "I thanked him."

"For what?" He said.

"For opening my eyes. For showing me the way."

"Always ready to help," Scott replied with a slight smile.

"Where are you going?" I asked.

"San Francisco, I'm going to San Francisco."

We embraced. A long, goodbye embrace.

"Perhaps I'll see you there someday. In San Francisco," I said.

"I'd like that." Then he turned and left. I was standing in the apartment we had shared for the last two years. It suddenly felt so empty.

I managed to find another roommate for my last year, but it was not the same. We didn't connect that way. And we didn't talk about it. "Finish college, and get on with it," I told myself.

And now I was, getting on with it. Moving to San Francisco.

New Mexico and then north to Utah. Utah. No way. All those Mormons. No way they'd accept me. I needed to get to San Francisco, where I was sure to find a community that would accept me. People who would share my same feelings. Yes, I would lose my feeling of isolation in San Francisco. Perhaps my anger too.

The smoke was drifting under my bedroom door. I opened the window. Too far to jump, I laughed. The fire engines were pouring water into the building. But not up to my floor. I was too high up. Damn it, why didn't I select the apartment on the first floor. No view, she said. I wanted the view and now I was paying for it.

I tried to contact Scott after he left. Called, left messages, but he never got back to me. I guess he's moved on to someone else, I thought.

I wasn't angry, just disappointed. Anyway, what difference did it make now with the snake knocking at my bedroom door.

I thought of my parents. We talked almost every Sunday. It was just talk. "How are you? How's the weather? Seen any good movies lately?" That kind of talk. Meaningless, filling up airtime. Never got around to what I wanted to say, what I had to say. And now. The snake would probably get me before I had the chance. Damn it. I so wanted to tell them.

Then I thought of Scott. The last time I saw him as he was leaving our apartment. Walking out of my life. Things I didn't say. That's what you remember, things you didn't say.

The bedroom door was on fire now. The wood was snapping. The snake was winning. Soon the whole damn bedroom would be in flames. Should I jump? Or just burn up? I didn't much care for either.

Certainly not like I cared for my parents. I loved them, but would they understand? Would they accept me now? And Scott, I cared for him in a different way. But what difference would it make now.

The bedroom door collapsed. I closed my eyes. "You win," I shouted to the snake.

"What?"

I opened my eyes.

"What did you say?" He was standing there. A fireman. He had knocked down the door. The snake was gone. I didn't say anything.

"Time to get you out of here." he said.

"Thank you."

Outside looking up at the charred structure, I felt the cell phone in my pocket.

I did have a chance to tell them, and I would do it now.

The phone rang. My dad answered.

"Hello, son, how are you? How's the weather in California?"

"Dad, please get mom and put me on the speaker phone."

"Sure, hold on."

I thought about what I wanted to say, how I would say it. I felt like I was coming out, at last."

"Hi, Billy, it's mom. Dad said you wanted to tell us something."

I cleared my throat and took a deep breath.

"Mom, dad, I've been wanting to tell you this for the longest time, but I was afraid how you would take it and whether you'd still love me."

"What is it son, don't be afraid to tell us."

"Yes, Billy, what is if?"

"Mom, dad, I've …". I stopped, could I finish?

"Yes, what son, tell us."

"I've left the Republican Party; I've become a Democrat."

There was a loud gasp at the other end of the line.

Then my dad spoke. "Seen any good movies lately?" They both were laughing. I started laughing too.

"No, but my apartment burnt down today."

"Are you okay?"

"Yes, I am and I'll tell you all about it this Sunday.

The phone disconnected. That went well, I thought. Better than I thought. Perhaps next week I can tell them about Scott and me. Yes, that would be nice too. I'll do it.

THE TIMEPIECE

IT WAS LIKE NO OTHER watch I had seen. I was intrigued.

"What is this?" I said about to pick it up.

"Oh, please do not touch. It is very …"

"Sorry, I was just curious."

"And understandably so."

He was cradling the watch in his hand, like some precious timepiece. Close enough for me to see, but not close enough for me to touch.

He had a curious accent. I couldn't place it and yet I considered myself well-traveled.

"What kind of watch is it?"

He broke out in a strange smile, not so much a friendly smile, more like you really don't want to know smile.

"One of a kind. Nothing like it."

His smile slowly fell away, revealing a random pattern of deep wrinkles and dark blemishes covering his face. The sun, I thought, he has spent a lot of time in the hot sun. Perhaps some small island in the South Pacific or a mountainous region in South America. The accent still had me guessing.

"Where was it made?" I asked, hoping an answer might provide me with a clue as to where the old man was from.

He shrugged his shoulders and tilted his head slightly but said nothing.

"How old is it, the watch?"

"Very old."

I could see I was getting nowhere with my questions, but the watch had me hooked. I wanted to know about it. It was more like I needed to know about it.

He was at the annual summer county fair. First time I had seen him there. Most vendors were here with their usual offerings, organic vegetables and fruits, first edition books, posters and post cards, cotton candy and lemonade. Then there were the animal displays, sheep, horses, pigs, and this year for the first time, a tall llama.

But the old man was new. He stood out, with his display table of stuff. Odd stuff. Like the watch.

"Are you from around here?" I asked, still trying to strike up a conversation.

"These parts? No, not at all."

"So where might you be from?"

"Just passing through," was his non-answer answer.

I figured him to be in his 70s. Tall and lank. Long, unkept grey hair, curling from under a beat-up L.A. Dodgers baseball cap.

"L.A.?" I pointed at the cap, "are you from Los Angeles?"

"This?"

As he removed the cap, I saw the big scar across the top of his forehead. I tried to look the other way.

"Yes, the Dodgers' baseball cap. Are you from L.A.?"

"Naa, I just found this."

He put the cap back on, adjusting the brim so the scar was no longer visible.

Jesus, I was getting nowhere with this guy. I should just walk away. Should, but I didn't. Couldn't.

"You have some mighty interesting stuff on your table," I said hoping some flattery would get him to open up.

"Guess so," was all I got.

Just then, a young couple approached the table. The girl was licking a snow cone and her fella was holding a bottle of beer. By his staggering, I suspected it wasn't his first.

"Hey, Debbie look what we have here," he said with a very noticeable slur.

"Holly shit, some really old stuff," she replied. Her voice suggested she had just moved on from her beer to the snow cone.

"How much for this old watch," the guy asked pointing at the timepiece.

"It's not for sale."

"But the sign on the table says everything's for sale."

"Yeah, everything." It was Debbie now, leaning over the table, her snow cone teetering dangerously above the items on the table.

The old man was clearly uncomfortable, probably angry too. He grabbed the watch and held it tight.

"No, no, not for you. Nothing on this table is for you."

The old man waved his hand, indicating he wanted the couple to leave. They didn't.

"What's your problem?"

"No problem, nothing on this table is for sale. Please leave."

The couple was not happy. Of course, all the beer didn't help their attitude.

"Well, fuck you, old man, they shouted, and then in an ominous tone, the guy, pointing directly at the old man, whispered, "watch out, we might be back."

"No doubt," the old man said, "no doubt."

As they left, the guy tossed his beer can in the direction of the old man.

The beer can was half full, so when it landed on the table, it doused most of the items in Coors Light. The timepiece was spared.

"Jesus, what was that all about?" I asked.

"What?"

"That. Throwing his beer. And threatening to come back."

"Oh, I guess he wants the watch."

"Yes, but he threatened you."

"I expected as much."

I stood there in disbelief trying to understand what I just saw and the old man's calm response. Expected that. Why would he say that?

"Are you going to call security?"

"It won't do much good," he replied, again in a very calm, matter of fact voice.

"What are you talking about?"

"Some things are just meant to be. That's all."

"But …"

"And you can't change the future, so why try?"

"But …"

"And if you could, the entire universe would be thrown out of balance. Chaos would take over. Nope, I ain't changing the future. No sir, not me. Not over a watch and certainly not over a damn beer."

My God, I thought, that was the most the old man had said all afternoon. But of course, I didn't understand a word he had said. Universe out of balance, changing the future. What the hell was that all about?

Then it occurred to me. My psychology class in college. Psych 101. A long time ago.

"So, no free will, is that it?"

His eyes suddenly lit up. A smile came over him. I had pulled him in.

"Exactly. You understand, don't you? You understand that free will is an illusion. You have no choice in how you act."

"Or how others act?" I injected.

"Yes, yes. Exactly."

"Kind of depressing, don't you think? No self-determination. We're just going through the motions."

"No, not at all."

"Oh."

"Yes, no free will means we don't have to assume any moral responsibility for our actions. We had no choice to do what we did."

"But …"

"So, when that guy comes back, and he will, whatever happens has already been determined. It is out of anyone's control."

"But, how do you know he will? Come back?"

His smile grew wider. Now he had pulled me in.

"The watch. This timepiece."

"Huh."

"It's more than a teller of the time. It's also a teller of the time in the future."

"What?"

"Yes, the future."

"But how?"

"If you wear it, you can set it ahead to whatever time you want. Once you do, you will actually be in the future. In that particular time in the future."

"No way. That's impossible."

He continued, moving closer to me. I could feel his warm breath on my face. I couldn't move.

"So, there's no free will. The future has been set. We're just waiting to catch up to it. For it to play out."

"I don't believe you. That's crazy."

"Do you want to put on the watch? Do you want to see the future? The future that's already happened!"

"That's crazy, You're crazy."

"Afraid to wear it. Afraid I'm telling the truth?"

He held the watch in his outstretched hand.

"Here, put it on. I've set it to just a few minutes from now."

I reached for the timepiece. I would play along with this. This joke.

"Sure, okay, I'll do it. Then we'll both have a good laugh when I do."

The watch was surprisingly light. As I tightened the band, a slight shock ran from my wrist up my arm.

But nothing looked different. I was still at the table with the old man. He was looking past me, with a slight smile on his face.

I turned in the direction he was looking.

It was them. The young guy with his girlfriend. He was carrying a gun.

"I told you I'd be back."

He was shouting. Angry. His girlfriend pushed him forward.

"Get him Jake. Shoot him, damn it. Shoot the old fart."

The gun exploded.

I heard a crash and turned in the direction of the table.

The old man was slumped over on the collapsed table. Blood ran over the tabletop and on to the dirt. It was like a small red stream slowly moving in my direction.

I looked at the young guy. He was laughing. So was his girlfriend. A crowd was gathering. I heard the sound of an approaching police car. The sun was setting. It was dusk. It was getting cold.

I looked at my wrist, at the timepiece.

I struggled with the band. I needed to remove it. I was in a panic now.

The timepiece fell to the ground.

"Hey, be careful with that." It was him, the old man.

He was standing behind his table.

Then, I heard her.

"Get him Jake. Shoot him, damn it. Shoot the old fart."

I turned and saw the gun.

I knew what I had to do.

I jumped between the old man and the gun.

The searing pain spread throughout my shoulder. I fell to the ground.

A security guard wrestled the young guy to the ground. His gun had fallen from his hand. Bystanders were running away. His girlfriend was sobbing.

The setting sun was still warm. I felt it on my face. I heard an ambulance approach.

The old man kneeled at my side. He was holding up my head.

"Jesus Christ, why did you do that?"

I looked him in the eyes and started to laugh.

"I guess I had to prove that Aristotle was correct."

He looked at me. He was confused. Now I had him.

"There is free will. Aristotle was right."

THE NORTH STAR

WE WERE STARING UP AT the night sky. The blanket beneath us hardly protecting us from the small rocks. We didn't care.

"The first one to see a shooting star, gets to make a wish," she said.

That was her favorite game. I knew it was and so I always made sure she saw the first one.

"Okay," I said, already aware of the outcome.

We were only 13 and thought we were in love. At least I thought we were. I also thought I knew what love was.

"There, there," she said, her voice rising with that excitement that almost made me laugh. But, of course, I didn't, because we were in love, and I didn't want to upset her.

"You saw it first again. Perhaps just one time I'll be first." I tried to insert a little disappointment in my voice. Not too much, of course.

"What did you wish for?" I asked.

"Oh, it's a secret. If I tell you, it might not come true. Probably won't."

That was always her answer. But I couldn't help but wonder. Did it have something to do with us? With me?

"Show me the North Star?" she asked, "please."

I glanced upward, looking for the familiar Big Dipper. Like ancient sailors, hundreds and hundreds of years ago, on uncharted waters, in search of new lands. Yes, I could have been one of those sailors, I thought. I could be the one looking for the North Star.

There it were the seven bright stars of the constellation Ursa Major. Four of them representing the bowl and three the handle.

"See that group of stars." I was pointing at them. "Can you imagine a dipper, with a handle and the bowl?"

"Oh yes, I do," she drew closer to me. I wanted to think she did that because we were in love, but then I thought, it is getting cold. Perhaps she was just getting cold.

"Tell me more," she continued.

"Well, now imagine the bowl is full of water.

"Or soup?" She offered.

"Yes, why not, chicken noodle soup."

I knew that was her favorite soup. Chicken noodle. I guess when you're in love, you just know these things about one another, I thought. Perhaps that's what love is? Perhaps I should ask my parents, because none of my friends knew.

"Now imagine you want to pour the water, er the chicken noodle soup, out of the dipper."

"Oh, this is so exciting," she said. "I love it when you tell me this story."

Love it, she always said, love it. But never, I love you when you tell me this story. I didn't know what to make of that. Did she love me, or did she just love my stories about the stars? Perhaps both? Yes, that would be nice.

"Keep pouring the soup. Pouring, pouring."

I too thought of the soup, pouring from the pointer stars of the Big Dipper. Just like those ancient sailors, I was convinced. Wondering if they thought of soup, or water, or something else pouring out of the dipper.

"Are you pouring your soup?" I asked.

I was slowly moving my hand, tracing our imaginary chicken noodle soup, pouring out of the Big Dipper. As I did, she did the same. Then our hands touched. Actually touched. I felt my heart jump. I said nothing. She just giggled. Was that a giggle of love, I thought?

"Do you see where the soup hits that very bright star."

"Yes, yes, I do," she said. She was laughing now, not at me, but a laugh of excitement having found Polaris."

"Well, that's Polaris, the North Star." I said, almost boasting about leading her to it. Then I felt guilt. I shouldn't be boasting. I can't imagine you should do that with someone you cared for.

We continued looking skyward into the moonless night. Not a cloud to block our view. Nor city lights either. The advantage of living in the countryside.

We were both silent now. I thought of when we first met. Our parents were enrolling us in the fifth grade at our new school.

After, the new students and their parents were seated in a large auditorium. It was there that they sat next to us. It was there that I first saw Judy.

"And this is our daughter, Judy." I heard the words, but I was too nervous to pay much attention. My heart was pounding.

My dad spoke, "Michael, please say hello to Judy."

"I brought myself back to the present. "Sorry, hi I'm Michael." I could feel the heat radiating from my face. I'm sure I had turned red. An embarrassing red.

Judy and I were in the same home room. She also lived close to our home, actually our farm.

Together, we walked to school and home after. Many times, I would stop at her house and her mom would invite me in. That's when I first had chicken noodle soup. We studied together. Although most of the time I wasn't studying. I just wanted to be with her. Close to Judy.

Fifth grade, sixth grade, and now we had just started seventh grade. We were no longer in the same home room, but that didn't matter, because we still walked to school together every morning. Judy and me.

It was getting colder now, but I was not ready to leave. I could stay here forever looking at the stars with Judy. Forever.

"Where's the belt?" She finally broke the silence.

"The belt?"

"Yes, you know the belt of origin."

"Oh, you mean the Belt of Orion."

"Yes, yes, Orion." She was laughing, almost uncontrollably. I started laughing too. Oh, this was so nice, here, together, laughing, looking for the Belt of Orion. With Judy. Yes, this, had to be love. It had to be.

She rolled over on her side. She was facing me. She was smiling. "Well?"

"Well, what?" I replied.

"Where is the belt?"

Oh, that I thought. I had forgotten all about that. I was so focused on her, her laughing, and her smile.

"We need to find three stars, in almost a straight line. Three bright stars. There are only three in the whole sky that are in a straight line. So, we need to hunt, like star detectives."

"First one to find them, gets a wish," she said.

"Sure," I said. I had already found them but would play the game with her. And of course, I knew how it would end. And that was okay.

"There, there." She jumped to her feet. "I found it."

"Congratulations, detective Judy."

She sat back down. Our legs touched. She was so warm. I could feel her through those long pants. I had goose bumps and was chilled. It was her, I thought. She's giving me the chills. Another sign of love?

"You know so much about the stars," she said. "Why?"

"It's been my hobby for a long time. I even built my own telescope," I replied, neglecting to say that I actually watched my dad put it together for me last Christmas. "I've always been interested in the stars, the planets, and especially the North Star."

"Why, the North Star?"

"Before the compass, sailors would find their way at sea with the help of the North Star. It was there in the night sky, pointing the way. Those ancient sailors found comfort when they saw that North Star, especially when they were sailing back home.

"Michael, you know so much. It's always fun to be with you."

"Thank you. I enjoy being with you too."

"I'll always remember these evenings, your stories, and looking for the North Star."

Always remember. What was she telling me? I was confused, my hands started shaking. My heart was racing. I was really cold now.

"Every time, I look into the night sky for the North Star, I'll think of you and chicken noodle soup."

I struggled to get out the words. "What are you saying?"

"We're moving, back home. Back to Australia."

I stood there, my hands at my side. Looking down at the ground. I didn't know what to say. Perhaps, there was nothing to say.

"We leave in a couple of days."

All I managed to say was, "oh."

She must have sensed my sadness. She came close and lifted my head up. Could she see the tears on my cheeks? Then she spoke. Softly.

"I will miss you so much. You, not just your stories. You."

Then she kissed me. On my lips. It was so soft. And then she pulled away.

I wanted to tell her I would miss her too. I wanted to tell her I thought I loved her. Yes, I was sure this was love, this is what it must have felt like. That feeling of doom, impeding emptiness, loneliness. I wanted to tell her.

I hesitated, I couldn't. Eventually, I did speak.

"You will not see it there."

"What?" What won't I see?"

"You'll be too far south, below the equator."

"And?"

"The North Star can't be seen that far south."

She turned back towards me. She was crying. She was waiting for me to say something. But I walked away instead.

That was my last night with Judy. Our last night with the North Star. I never saw her again. She left for Australia two days later.

I was sixty-five now and still I wondered why I didn't tell her. Damn it, I should have. Was I angry at her for leaving me? Yes, but still I should have told her. But it was too late now. I would never have the chance.

When she was standing there, crying, that's when I could have said it. I could tell she was upset. It would have been so easy for me to have told her.

"Don't cry Judy. While you won't see the North Star, you can see the Southern Cross. Find it and follow it to the South Star. When you do, think of me. I'll do the same with the North Star."

But I didn't. I still look for the North Star. But now it's like any other star in the night sky. It's not our special star. Never again.

BARBERSHOP THERAPY

"**Y**OU'RE UP NEXT, JOHN."

"Huh?"

I was reading the latest edition of Sporting World. Wilt Chamberlain scored 100 points in a basketball game last night.

It was March 3, 1962.

"You're up. Chair's empty."

"Oh yeah."

"Of course, I can take Sammy if you prefer."

"No, no, sorry, Robert."

Robert was tall and thin, in his early 80s, a good friend for the last 30 years. Maybe my best friend. He was also my barber.

"Well then get your black butt over here."

It was the Smoking Barber Shop, in the middle of black Harlem, in upper Manhattan.

Harlem. Originally a Dutch village, formally organized in 1658, named after the city of Haarlem in the Netherlands.

In the 19th century, Harlem was occupied mainly by Jewish and Italian Americans. However, in the early 20th century African-Americans began to arrive and they did so in large numbers.

The influx of African-Americans into Harlem was part of the Great Migration, one of the largest movements of people in United

States. Black southerners relocated to northern and midwestern cities including, New York, Chicago, Detroit, and Pittsburgh.

While the driving force behind the Great Migration was escaping racial violence and the oppression of southern Jim Crow laws, many came north looking for better jobs.

By the 1930s, Harlem had become a predominantly black neighborhood. That's when I arrived, from Alabama, at the age of 18.

The Smoking Barber Shop was where I got my first haircut. And that's where I met Robert. My barber and more. Much more. So much more.

In Alabama, as the Mexican boll weevil took its toll on the state's cotton fields, I looked north for a better life and a better paycheck. But at 18, I struggled with my transition from the lazy cotton fields of the Alabama Black Belt Prairie region to the fast pace of Harlem.

In an astonishingly short amount of time, the neighborhood of Harlem became the center of Black culture in America.

The cultural movement, referred to as the Harlem Renaissance, attracted authors, artists, musicians, and political activists who explored black culture. W.E.B. DuBois, a co-founder of the National Association for the Advancement of Colored People, was among the leading intellectuals of the renaissance. Langston Hughes, considered among the greatest poets in U.S. history, was known for poetry that demonstrated jazz-like rhythm. Louis Armstrong often played at speakeasies in Harlem while Duke Ellington performed at the famous Cotton Club.

No wonder that Harlem had become known as the "black capital" of America.

"You new to Harlem, boy? I ain't seen you here before." It was Robert, it was 1931, and I just eased into his tall leather barber chair. My hands gently settled on the cool porcelain arm rests.

I felt at home.

"Yes, sir. First week here." I replied.

"From?"

"Alabama, sir. Monroe, Alabama."

"Have you found work.?"

"Not yet."

"Well, you might check with Evan's grocery store down the block. I heard they're looking for stockers."

"Thanks, I will."

"And tell them Robert sent you."

"Sure will Ro ..."

I coughed as I realized I was about to call him by his first name.

"I mean, sir."

"Robert's okay, but never call me Bob. Never."

His large hand was on my shoulder, and I could feel the slight tightening as he repeated,

"Never."

"Okay, sir ... I mean Robert."

"And you? Your name?"

"Johnny, but most people call me John."

"Okay John, let's take care of that wild head of hair."

At that moment, Robert and I connected.

Over the years we became friends, good friends. But never equal. He was always the older, wiser Robert, and I the kid from Monroe, Alabama.

And that was okay with me.

But Robert wasn't just a friend. He was also a great listener.

Barbershops, especially in Black communities like Harlem, were seen as a safe, nonjudgmental space for men to talk about anything— sports, politics, religion, women, manhood. The Smoking Barber Shop was no exception.

Like most black barbers of his time, Robert practiced barbershop therapy. He used to joke that he probably should be charging for both the haircut and the therapy session. While he joked about it, the service he provided to black men was invaluable.

I once asked Robert why his clients looked at him as a therapist.

"Easy," he said. "When they come to me for a haircut, they're trusting me with their most prized possession, their hair. So, if they trust and respect me to cut their hair, then they can trust and respect me to help them with their problems."

I often wondered if it was really that simple.

But whatever the reason, I found myself checking into Robert's barbershop therapy throughout the 30 years I lived in Harlem.

"100 points? How did he do that?" It was Robert.

"Jesus Christ, Robert, it was Wilt Chamberlain. I'm surprised it wasn't 200 points."

Slapping his large comb against the top of my head, Robert whispered,

"No swearing in here, John. Remember the rules."

The rules. No swearing was rule number 1, followed by whatever is said in the shop, remains in the shop. Rule three, tell the truth. Final rule, never call Robert, Bob. Those were the rules. Four of them.

"Sorry, Robert, but damn I'm still surprised he didn't score 200, maybe 300."

Robert started laughing. That unique laugh of his. A cross between a chuckle and a snort. And when he did, you knew all was good again between you and him.

"How much we taken off today?" It was Robert, holding a hair pick in one hand and his clippers in the other.

I looked at the hair pick, and it took me back to the first time I sat in the barber chair at the Smoking Barber Shop. I had never seen one before. It looked like a large fork, and I couldn't imagine what it as used for.

"Excuse me, sir, but what's that thing?" I asked Robert.

"Just a pick, boy. Why, you never seen one?"

"Never."

"Well, son, lucky you came to a black barber, 'cause we know our hair is different."

"Huh?"

"Yeah, black men's hair is naturally curly and tends to tangle. So, I use this pick to remove tangles before cutting. Otherwise, you'd end up looking like a rag doll, or worse."

"Didn't know that."

"My goodness, boy, didn't you ever go to a barber shop in Alabama?"

I hesitated to answer. Embarrassed to tell him that my mom always cut my hair. She couldn't afford to send me to a real barber. So, she cut my hair with the household scissors. No pick thing. Just the slightly dull household scissors.

So, I lied.

"Of course, I been. Went to the best in Monroe."

Robert didn't say anything. But by his looks I could tell that he knew I was fibbing. Probably because my hair looked like a rag doll as I made my way to his barber chair.

That was the first and last time I lied to Robert.

"Barbershop therapy don't work if you don't tell the truth," Robert would say to distraught customers. "Rule three. Open up, tell me what's going on."

And so, I did. Over the next 30 years, Robert was my go-to therapist.

He listened to me and provided advice on so many issues. Dealing with gang pressure, on asking a girl out, proposing to my wife to be, frustrations with my job, dealing with sorrow, and life in general. Robert, and his barbershop therapy, was also there, even when I thought I didn't need it.

And today, as I eased into the barber chair the day after Wilt Chamberlain scored 100 points, I needed it more than ever. I just didn't know how much.

"So, John, how much we taken off today."

"You decide, Robert."

"One of those days, huh."

Robert was also good at interpreting the tone in one's voice. I guess he could tell something was bothering me.

"Wanta talk about it."

"Don't think so, not today."

"Well, whatever pleases you."

Robert was also good at getting one to open up. It was that soothing voice of his. No pressure, whatever pleases you approach.

I took a deep breath,

"It's Shawn, my son Shawn." I said softly.

Robert didn't say anything. It was his way of encouraging me to continue.

He was using the pick to untangle my hair, but I knew he was listening to every word. And thinking.

"Ever since his mom passed, our relationship has gone south."

The pick snagged on an uncooperative tangle.

"Ouch."

"Sorry, John." It was that soothing voice that made me want to continue.

"The crowd he's running around with now is just going to get him in trouble, and worse probably."

I paused, but still Robert didn't respond.

"He was staying with us ever since his mom got sick, and even after."

My throat suddenly tightened up. But I had to continue.

"Last night ... last night, we had a terrible argument, and ..."

Robert had the clippers now and he was starting to cut my hair.

"And what, John?"

Perfect timing, I thought. As usual, he knows when to ask questions.

"I asked him to leave, to get out of the house, and to ... to get out of my life."

"How did Shawn take it?"

"He just stormed out. Slammed the door and drove away."

"And you? How are you dealing with it?"

"Okay, I think. I just couldn't deal with him anymore."

Robert put down the clippers as he walked around to the front of the barber chair. Placing his hands on my shoulders, he said,

"Can I tell you a story?"

"Of course."

"When I was a young teenager, my dad decided to abandon his family. Not sure why. He just up and left.

"Later he was arrested for armed robbery and was sent to jail. He never got out as he was stabbed to death during a prison riot."

"Did you ever see him after he left you?"

"I saw him once when he was in prison. I was probably Shawn's age at that time."

Robert picked up the clippers and walked behind me. The buzz of the clippers broke the silence.

"It was a very difficult meeting, but I felt I had to do it, felt I had to tell him something."

I looked in the mirror and saw Robert's reflection. That contagious smile was gone.

"I told him how I wished he had been there for me. How it wasn't fair to grow up without a dad, not to have a father in my life."

Suddenly I realized what Robert was telling me to do.

I wanted to tell him, to thank him, but as I looked back at his reflection, I saw tears dropping from his eyes.

Wiping them away, he said one word,

"Bob."

"What?"

"Bob. My dad's name was Bob."

THE BATTLEFIELD

THE WAR WAS COMING TO an end. At least we hoped so.

I was in a trench. My shoes were full of mud. My socks were wet. And I was cold. Damn cold. Jimmy could tell.

"Would you like some coffee?"

He was my good buddy, Jimmy.

"No thanks, I'm all coffeed out."

Jimmy and I had enlisted together. Enlisted was not the right word. We were drafted. Drafted into this crazy war.

I was on our farm in Pennsylvania when the letter came. U.S. Army, Official Business. My mother wanted to throw it away without opening it. My father said I needed to go.

"For the good of the country," he said.

Jimmy got his letter a few days later.

"But I could use another cigarette."

"Sure, let me roll one for you."

Ever since I got that damn infection in my right hand, I couldn't roll my cigarettes. The doctor said, "it will either heal itself, or your hand will fall off."

Jesus Christ, I didn't sign up to lose my right hand. Oh wait, I didn't sign up.

"Thanks doc," I said sarcastically, "thank goodness I'm left-handed."

He shrugged his shoulders, as he moved on to the next wounded soldier.

It had rained for three straight days. After a day we all gave up trying to stay dry.

"Well, at least it reduced the shootings," the captain had said.

The shooting, Jesus the shooting. Another soldier told me, "if you can hear them, it's a good thing, because when you don't hear them, you've probably been shot and are dead."

I didn't know what to say. Probably best I didn't say anything because the next day he didn't hear that bullet coming.

The morning sun was breaking through the overcast. I stood up slowly. Peering over the ridge of the trench, I saw them, through the lifting fog. More soldiers who had not heard the shot. Jesus, how long had they been lying out there?

"Best to get back down," Jimmy said with a smile, "you don't want to get your head blown off."

"I wonder if we're having food today?" I replied.

"I heard we're having steak and baked potatoes."

Jimmy was always a joker, even out here, where I thought there was so little to joke about. But occasionally, I tried.

"I'd like my steak rare and my potatoes with extra butter."

Jimmy just looked at me. Oh well, I tried, I thought.

Butter, oh for fresh butter. On our farm, we had plenty of fresh butter. Milk too. What I would give for a fresh glass of cold milk right now. And to be home, in Pennsylvania.

The captain came walking towards us. "Men," he said, "there may be a truce. We'll know shortly."

Men did he say? Hardly men. Mostly boys in their late teens. Probably few had had a beer, or kissed a girl. Jesus, men? What the hell is he thinking?

Well, I had kissed her. Mary Lou. Many times. We even tried doing it once, but her folks came home early. We had planned on getting married, but then this damn war broke out. Mary Lou, my sweet Mary Lou.

"What are your plans after this war?" Jimmy asked. "I bet it involves Mary Lou."

Rumor had it that Jimmy liked Mary Lou. A lot. She was the only pretty girl in the state of Pennsylvania, he used to say. I would always reply, "well, I got there first. So, I guess you'll have to move to New Jersey."

"Gonna get married. Buy a ranch. I want to raise cattle. I understand the market for beef is really good in the big cities, especially New York."

"Kids?" Jimmy asked.

"Oh yea, Mary Lou wants plenty of kids." I made sure the name Mary Lou rolled slowly out of my mouth. I wanted to make sure Jimmy heard it.

"And what are you doing, Jimmy?"

"I guess I'm moving to New Jersey." He laughed, but I couldn't tell if he was joking. Well, I guess he heard her name, I thought.

"Men," the captain was shouting now. "A truce had been reached. The war will be over at 12 noon."

Everyone was cheering. A few hats were thrown in the air. Someone fired their rifle.

"What time is it, captain?" one of the soldiers shouted. The captain was the only one with a watch. A few minutes until noon. Stay put. Stay safe, brothers.

Brothers, we're all brothers, I thought. Sure, some from the north, some from the south. I guess I never understood what this war was all about. The Union? The Confederacy? I was just a farmer. I'm sure some of the guys fighting for the south were farmers just like me.

Yes, we were all brothers.

For the nation, my dad said. Something about slavery, secession. Meant nothing to me. I just wanted to farm and be with Mary Lou.

Just then the captain started counting down. 30, 29, 28, 27 ....

Some of us started cheering.

Then Jimmy stood up.

"Wait, Jimmy," I screamed.

But he didn't hear me, and he didn't hear the bullet. He fell backwards into the trench, into the mud.

15, 14, 13, 12...

"What the hell, Jimmy. Why did you do that?"

I started crying. I stood up, "this is all shit."

Then I heard it. A whistling sound. Like the bumble bees back on our farm. I felt it too. So soft and warm at first, just like Mary Lou's kisses. But then it stung. It must have been a bumble bee sting I thought.

3, 2, 1, Zero.

They were wrong. But how could they know?

The blood poured down my face, covering my muddy boots. I started to fall backwards. I could hear cheering.

The war was over, and they were wrong. Dead wrong. You could definitely hear it and you could feel it.

JOHNNY AND NO NAME

MY SHIFT WAS OVER, AND it was dark outside. An hours drive to my apartment and then another lonely evening preparing dinner and watching TV. Perhaps I'll have a glass of wine tonight to celebrate the weekend. I might even open the good bottle of wine, that $2 red from Trader Joe's.

A slight rain, more like a mist, was falling as I pulled out of the company parking lot. The narrow winding road home is bad enough when it's light and dry, I thought. And now this, dark and wet.

At least there were few cars on the road. Steering around a curve and coming on to the one long straight stretch on my way home, I adjusted my headlights to high. Then I saw them in the distance.

Walking along the side of the road, with their backs to me, a man, and a dog. As I got closer, their shadows from my headlights stretched almost to the next curve.

Suddenly, the rain intensified. My old windshield wipers struggled to clear the windshield. Damn, why didn't I replace them last month, I thought, straining to see through the streaks. Straining to see the two figures ahead of me. I slowed the car to a crawl.

He was hitchhiking. I could see that. Holding a backpack above his head, trying to stay dry. His dog hung close to his side, trying to stay dry too,

My windshield wipers continued to grind against the glass. That

God awful grinding. The large raindrops were pinging on the roof of the car.

He was an older guy, with a shaggy beard. In need of a haircut, too. I wondered what he was doing out here on this less traveled road. Where he and his dog going on this rainy night?

Should I stop, I thought? I never picked up hitchhikers. Never felt comfortable enough. Didn't really like strangers either. But then,

My foot gently hit the brakes. Jesus, I was going to do it this time. I was stopping for the hitchhiker and his dog. I was really stopping.

"Need a ride?"

"Well, thanks we sure could use one. Especially in this downpour."

"Hop in. You can put you dog in the back along with your backpack."

He opened the back door and his dog jumped in, violently shaking the rain from his wet hair.

"Sorry about that. If you have a towel, I can clean it up."

"That's okay. It's only water. You better get in before you get soaked too."

As he slid into the passenger's seat, I saw his dirty pants and torn jacket. Shoes, but no socks. He was shivering.

"I can turn on the heat." I said.

"That would be nice. Thanks."

We rode in silence for a while. His dog fell asleep.

"Mind if I smoke," he finally said.

I hesitated to answer. After all, I hated the smell of cigarette smoke, and no one ever smoked in my car. But then,

"Sure, go ahead."

Jesus, why did I say that? Why was I letting this stranger light up a cigarette in my car?

"Would you like one?"

"What?"

"A cigarette. I rolled them myself this morning."

"No thanks, I'm trying to quit."

God, why did I say that? I've never smoked a day in my life.

"I should too, but can't seem to break the habit."

The rain was letting up now. The pinging and grinding were letting up too.

"Are you from around here?" I asked.

"Oh no, just passing through."

"To where? Where you going?"

"Don't know yet."

"Well, where you from?"

"Just got out of the army. I was discharged."

"Oh!"

"Yea, dishonorable discharge."

"Oh."

"Got in a fight with the company commander. Broke his nose. I lost a few teeth, but I got the best of him.

Oh Christ, who have I let in my car, I thought. Why did I stop?

Suddenly the dog started barking.

"Shut up. Shut up, or I'll throw you out of the car. Then you'll be on your own again. Damn it, shut up."

"Name?"

"What?"

"What's your dog's name?" I asked, trying to ease the rising tension in the car.

"Don't know. Just came across him one night when I was searching through a trash can for food. He's been with me ever since."

"Oh."

"No Name."

"Huh."

"I call him No Name."

"Oh."

"And you?" I asked. What should I call you?"

"Johnny. You can call me Johnny."

"Nice to meet you, Johnny."

"And you? What's your name?"

Again, I hesitated. Do I really want to give him my name? Should I make one up? But then I told him. Jesus, I actually told him.

"Nancy. My name's Nancy."

"You hungry, Nancy?"

"Yeah, a little."

"Well, I saw a sign for a steak house back there. It should be coming up soon."

I said nothing. Does this guy expect me to buy him dinner, I thought? A ride in my car was one thing. But buying him a steak, no way.

"My treat, Nancy. It'll be my treat. I insist. I want to thank you for picking us up. No Name and me."

The parking lot was almost full.

"Must be good," he said, "let's try it, Nancy."

Jesus, what am I doing? Going into this restaurant with this guy. Dishonorably discharged guy who befriended a dog while he's going through a trash can looking for food. And calls him No Name. I should let him out of the car, him and No Name, and be on my way. But then,

"Sure, why not. Shall we leave No Name in the car?"

"Yeah, I'll bring him some of my leftovers. He'll be fine until we get back."

We got out of the car and started walking towards the restaurant. Johnny put his hand on my shoulder.

"I'm sure glad you stopped, Nancy," he said. "I think we make a good couple. Yes, I do."

I didn't answer, but I didn't pull away either. Jesus, what am I doing, I thought? This isn't like me.

Entering the restaurant, the owner noticed us and quickly came over.

"I'm sorry sir, but we have a dress code."

Johnny looked directly at him. God, is he going to hit him? Another dishonorable discharge moment, I wondered."

"I'm sure you do, but I just returned from a tour of duty in a war zone overseas and I haven't had a chance to buy some new clothes. My wife here just picked me up at the military airport and we are headed home. Thought it would be nice to have a real meal for the first time in months. So, we stopped."

"Sorry I didn't realize your situation. Of course, you can eat here. All veterans are welcomed at my restaurant."

As we were shown to our table, Johnny turned to me with a big smile, "See honey, I told you it would be okay."

Jesus, what's with this guy. Wife. Honey. Now I'm his wife and his honey. I really need to get away from him. But then,

"Sure Johnny. This'll be great."

The steaks were cooked to perfection. An expensive bottle of wine too. Trader Joe's will never be the same, I thought.

Johnny was almost finished when he winked at me and pulled close.

"Are you ready to skip out?"

"What?"

"Leave this place."

"Without paying?"

"Of course, I don't have money."

"Well, let me pay."

"No way. Just follow my lead."

"What lead? What do you want me to do?"

"For starters throw that glass of water in my face and then run when I tell you."

"You're crazy, Johnny."

"Yes, perhaps but aren't you at all curious."

Hell no, I thought. Why would I want to do this? Jesus, we could get arrested. I could lose my job. But before I could answer him, Johnny stood up and started shouting.

"Damn it, Nancy. I go to war, and you start an affair with my best friend." He was screaming. "Being my wife meant nothing to you. How could you." He started pounded the table with his fists. Dishes crashed to the floor.

Everyone in the restaurant stopped what they were doing and looked at us. No one moved.

"I should kill you and him," Johnny screamed. "I can't believe you carried on like that."

Johnny nodded at the glass of water in front of me. "I go off to war and you and Joe go off screwing. How could you, Nancy, how could you do this to me?"

I reached for the glass of water. Johnny mouthed the word now. With one swift motion I picked up the glass and tossed the water at his face.

"You better run, bitch. I'm coming for you."

Johnny pulled a gun from under his shirt and pointed at me. "You better run. Both you and Joe."

And I did, as fast as I could, through the restaurant, knocking over chairs and out the front door. Johnny followed, waving his gun. No one stopped him. No one dared.

The tires spun as we exited the parking lot.

"Jesus, Johnny. I can't believe you, we, did that."

"Exciting, huh?"

Again, I hesitated. I could feel my heart racing. My hands were shaking. I was almost out of breath. Exciting. Jesus, yes it was, I thought.

"God yes, Johnny. What a rush."

"Just the beginning. Would you like more?"

"Johnny, I can't. I have a job, an apartment, a ..."

"Boyfriend?"

I hesitated again. Hardly a boyfriend, I thought. An occasional dinner, perhaps a movie, unsatisfying sex, that's for sure.

"Yea, a boyfriend."

"What's his name, Nancy?"

I hesitated, then I responded.

"No Name, I call him No Name." We both broke out in laughter.

"Job. What about your job? Exciting job."

"Well, it pays the rent, food bill too."

"But exciting?"

My job, I thought. Hardly exciting. Assembly line work. Putting together car seats for babies. Eight hours a day. Jesus, the hour at the restaurant was more exciting than all the ten years on the assembly line.

"No."

"So, what's holding you back?"

I hesitated one last time. Nothing, I thought, nothing is holding me back. But was I ready for this? Ready for Johnny and No Name? But then,

"Nothing Johnny. Nothing's holding me back."

The car accelerated into the night. We passed my dark apartment. No turning back now, I thought.

The storm was over. No Name was awake. We were heading east. The sun was rising in the sky ahead of us.

"New day," Johnny said.

"What should we do today?" I asked.

"Oh, I don't know. Perhaps we'll rob a bank or two."

Okay, now I knew I had made a mistake. Running out of a restaurant without paying is one thing but robbing a bank. Now that's serious. I mean I could get killed. But then,

"Hey, Johnny, could I have one?"

"One what, Honey?"

"One of those cigarettes.

LIKE HAIR STUCK IN BUTTER

THE HORSES STRUGGLED IN THE snow. The wagons they were pulling were loaded. Supplies, and, of course, people with all the household items and important possessions they could load.

Up to this point, the journey had been relatively easy. Well, except for the bad dust storms in Kansas. Two wagons actually turned back.

"A sign from the devil," they said as they turned around to the east.

I was beginning to think that maybe they were right. The devil. It was a sign from Lucifer himself.

Stopping in the deep snow this night at the top of the pass. The horses were exhausted, as were we.

"Best not to continue under these conditions in the dark." It was the wagon master, Jake. A tall lanky guy from Colorado. He had made this trip many times so that's why we hired him.

Jake confessed yesterday that the last few days were turning out to be the most difficult ones of all of the trips he had led.

"Let's stop for the night and decide what to do in the morning."

Decide? What did that mean? We couldn't go back. Not with those gunslingers behind us. We were lucky to lose them when we reached the trailhead. Surely, they'd be waiting for us and our supplies if we returned. Just waiting to get the drop on us if we showed up. Nope, we weren't going back.

So, we'd either be waiting out a change in the weather or attempting to make our way down the valley. Down the valley and into California. Where we all wanted to settle. To start a new life.

At two miles an hour we figured the 2,000-mile trip from Missouri to California would take about five or six months, but with these snowstorms, probably closer to nine.

"Right now, I just want to make sure I keep you all above the snakes," Jake said.

Jake looked at us and could see we were confused, as usual. "Above the snakes," he repeated with a chuckle, "just trying to keep you greenhorns alive, above the snakes."

Cowboys. It was like they had their own language, I told Martha, my wife. She just smiled and shook her head.

"Grub up." It was Jake again, informing us that it was time to eat. At least we knew that expression.

We were down to four wagons after the two left us in Kansas. Four wagons. Twelve of us plus Jake. We decided early on to have our meals together, at least dinner. Each night a different wagon would prepare the meal. Of course, Jake was the exception.

Tonight, preparing meals would be especially difficult, so Jake said he would cook, and we would meet by his wagon for dinner. This was a first.

"Hey Jake, this is really good. What is it?" It was Martha.

"Chuck wagon chicken."

"Really. It doesn't taste like chicken."

"That's cause it ain't. It's bacon."

And so, it was like that, all across the Great Plains, over the Rocky Mountains, and now at the peak of Donner Pass in the northern Sierra Nevada Mountains looking west to California. Cowboy slang. Almost like a daily lesson. But I suspect we still had a lot to learn.

The approach from the east to the 7,000-foot summit was steep and treacherous, but even in the raging snowstorm we made it without incident.

But now we were facing a difficult decision. The drop into California was gradual, but the problem was the deep heavy snow at the peak. The wagons wouldn't budge. The horses couldn't pull them.

The next morning conditions had not improved, and if anything, perhaps it had gotten worse with the snow last night.

Jake was up early, brewing the morning coffee.

"Morning, Jake. How's it looking today?" I asked.

Jake looked up and smiled, "Like a hair stuck in the butter."

Well, this was definitely a new one for me, hair in the butter, but not too difficult to figure out. Like a hair stuck in butter, I suspect we weren't going anywhere today.

"Would you like some coffee?" Now it was Jake's turn to ask a question.

"Huh?"

"Coffee, would you like some coffee?"

"Oh, you mean an Arbuckle's?" I replied. I was holding a can of the popular brand of coffee that cowboys used in place of the word coffee. Arbuckle's.

"You learn fast," Jake said. "Here's your Arbuckle's."

Weeks passed, the weather was getting slightly better, but Jake insisted we stay at the summit.

"That's a dog that won't hunt," Jake would say whenever we asked if we'd be leaving soon. "You'll end up in a bone orchard if we attempt to descend now."

As we trusted Jake, at first no one questioned his decision to stay. But as the days grew warmer, some started grumbling.

"Why doesn't Jake want to leave. Doesn't he know we're running low on food?"

For a long time, I stood up for Jake and supported his decision, until that day when some of the travelers felt weak. That's when I decided to confront him.

"Jake. Can we talk."

"Sure."

"Have you noticed that the folks in wagon 3 seem to be ill, weak."

"Oh, I figured they were just off the feed. Didn't feel like eating."

"No Jake, they don't have much of anything to feed on. They've run out of food and the rest of us are getting mighty low too."

"Oh."

"We need to get moving or find some food, before we all starve."

"It'll be fine, trust me."

"But, Jake…"

"Trust me, I know what I'm doing. You need to be set with that. Okay?"

"Not sure, Jake. We're suffering. Soon, real soon, we'll all be too weak to travel. To make it down the mountain to California."

Jake looked at me and smiled. It was a strange smile. Not a smile one would expect from a friend. Then he said,

"Can I tell you a story?"

"I guess."

"It was about 25 years ago, right here on Donner Pass."

He looked around like he was taking in the pass. Admiring the pass.

"Right here, this very spot. Five wagons on their way to California were stranded at the peak. Terrible conditions. Stranded for weeks."

"Like this, Jake?"

"Almost. Snow and blizzards. Couldn't move."

"But the snow is melting, Jake. Our conditions are not like you describe."

"Sure, they are. Wagons stuck in the snow at the top of the pass." He was raising his voice. "The same."

"But …"

"So, you know what they had to do?"

"No Jake, I don't."

"They resorted to cannibalism to survive."

"They what?"

"Well, first the horses, and then their fellow travelers."

"Jesus Jake, what are you telling me?"

"And it was because of him, the wagon train leader that some survived and made it to California."

Jake was paying no attention to me. He was so into his story. The group had gathered around to listen.

"Him, Alfred Packer. He saved them. He forced them to accept cannibalism."

"Jake, Jake, who is this Packer? Alfred Packer?"

"My father, of course. Who did you think?"

"And you?"

"I was only ten at the time. Ten. Here on Donner Pass. Here at that time, with my father."

"Jesus Jake, did you eat ..."

"Ate it, and..." Jake smacked his lips, "loved it. Couldn't get enough."

We all looked at one another. Jake was laughing, but it wasn't a pleasant laugh, then he spoke,

"And after you try it, you'll be hooked."

"But Jake ..."

"And you can thank me later, but right now just consider yourselves a hair stuck in the butter."

THE DREAM CATCHER

THEY APPEARED AS BRIGHT RED and orange bands against a light gray backdrop. Low in the early morning sky.

Slowly the entire sky to the east was ablaze with the color of gold. The sun had risen. It was a new day.

I had spent the last few hours of darkness in the old truck, on a bluff overlooking the canyon. The towering sandstone rock formations soaring up to 1,000 feet above the valley floor were wakening from the darkness of night. I never grew tired of seeing them. I felt they were talking to me. Telling me stories of my ancestors.

I was on the Navajo Nation reservation in southern Utah, in Monument Valley Navajo Tribal Park, or Tse'Bii'Ndzisgaii, the Valley of the Rocks, as my people first called this place longer back than any of us could remember.

The dream catcher came into focus. Hanging from the rear-view mirror. A circular willow hoop, its center woven into a net, like a spider's web, with leather streamers tied to the hoop.

According to Shimá Sání, my maternal grandmother, night air was filled with good and bad dreams. The dream catcher was a protective talisman, as the web would trap bad dreams, while the circle in its center would allow good dreams and visions to pass through.

"But why a spider and its web," I had asked her.

Shimá Sání smiled as she replied.

"A long time ago, before our memories started, Na'ashjé'iitsoh, the Spider Woman, weaved the web that became the universe. Then she decided to become the helper and protector of humans. She taught our people how to weave, to create rugs, how to create beauty. She is the source of all our artistic abilities. She taught us balance within the mind, body, and soul."

Then her smile turned serious as she continued, emphasizing each word as she spoke.

"Spider Woman can also cast her web like a net to capture and eat misbehaving children. She lives atop Spider Rock, which has turned white from the bleached bones of misbehaving children."

"You must respect all spiders and be careful not to kill them."

That was the first and last time I asked her about spiders.

However, from that day on, I made sure to avoid spiders and although I misbehaved on occasion, Na'ashjé'iitsoh never decided to capture and consume me.

And so, the dream catcher, with its spider web, which my grandmother made and hung above my crib so many years ago, now hung from my rear-view mirror.

I returned my vision to the vast valley before me.

The red sandstone pillars, standing as isolated hills with their steep, vertical sides and small, flat tops, were casting their early morning shadows across the desert floor. The shadows moved slowly like old Navajo men hunting for food.

Created over millions of years through the process of erosion, these majestic pillars were sacred to Navajos.

The very earliest Navajos had given these sacred pillars names, like Yei'bi'chei, but of course, those names had been replaced by later settlers to the valley. Now they were called by their shapes like the East and West Mittens, Three Sisters, Thunderbird Mesa, and so on.

Growing up, my family was one of ten families who lived inside the park. We did so in traditional shelters called hogans, which were constructed of wooden poles, tree bark and mud. As with our early ancestors, the only entrance to the single room hogan opened to the east, to greet the morning sun and receive its blessings. Without running water or electricity, life was difficult, but we managed to survive on farming and grazing for income. And we had each other.

As my grandmother told us, it was all part of our living in harmony with Mother Earth, Father Sky, and the many other earthly elements such as humans, animals, plants, and insects. It was taught to us many centuries ago by the Holy People, how to live the right way and how to conduct the many acts of everyday life.

This was my life. And I loved it. And I didn't want it to end.

Over the years, other residents had joined us in the valley. Wild horses, wild dogs, and even wild cows roamed the desert floor in search of food. Due to the extreme dryness and lack of moisture in the valley, vegetation consisted mainly of scattered juniper trees and purple sage, rabbitbrush, and Mojave yucca. Over time the valley's limited vegetation forced these new arrivals to raid our gardens for their daily meals.

Especially our corn. They loved corn.

For us, the Navajo, corn is the most revered of all plants. Growing straight and tall, corn resembles human beings standing in rows. White corn is thought to be male, yellow corn, female. Food made from corn, especially cornmeal, is symbolic of the goodness of Mother Earth and Father Sky.

Every spring, we planted large fields of corn. Not only was corn an essential food item, but it was also an important part of our ceremonies as a blessing and was always offered in prayer.

"Shoot them, son," my dad hollered. And we did. Especially the wild dogs.

I had been out this morning before sunrise to observe wild animals.

For hours I watched, but none appeared.

The only thing that had come into view were the bright stars, the full moon and the dream catcher hanging from the rear-view mirror.

The dream catcher, like the full moon, represented the circle of life to Navajos. The phases of the moon and the round shape of the dream catcher reminded our people of the changing nature of life. A beginning, a middle, an end, and then starting all over with a new beginning. Through millennia the repeating circle of life itself, of birth, living, and death.

I stepped out of the truck. As I did my grandmother's necklace of hardened corn kernels fluttered in the wind against my bare neck.

The blowing sand had covered the truck with a thin layer of fine red sand. There was no need to clean it, as the daily winds would simply cover it again. Everyone drove a sand covered vehicle. Well almost everyone. Newcomers would try to wash them, but soon, like us, they would surrender to the relentless winds. It was all part of accepting the behavior of Mother Earth my grandmother had told me.

The towering East and West Mittens were directly ahead. Two giant mitten shaped buttes reaching upward to the morning sky.

According to my grandmother, the two mittens were the mittens of the gods. They left them here in the valley, in what we called the playground of the gods, expecting some day they would come back and reclaim them. She never told me why. Why they needed mittens.

I wanted to ask her. Many times.

But I waited too long to ask her about the mittens. Soon she became old, and her last breath approached. Before it did, she was taken to a separate place to die.

When I asked mother why Shimá Sání had to leave, she said if grandma had died in our hogan, then our only dwelling would have to be torn down, destroyed. We would need to build a new one.

I was confused as to why, so mother explained that we had to take certain precautions so Shimá Sání's journey to the underworld would be smooth and uneventful. Because of the presence of evil spirits surrounding her at the time of her death, she needed to be moved from the hogan. When she was moved only a few individuals were to come in contact with her. And I was not to be one of them.

Mother continued.

After death, two older men were entrusted with preparing my grandmother's body for burial. They did not wear clothing during this process, they only wore their moccasins. Before starting the process, they rubbed ash all over their bodies, believing the ash would protect them from evil spirits.

All of this, my mother said, was to ensure that my grandmother didn't return to the living.

When I ask why we wouldn't want Shimá Sání to return, she only said she might unknowingly bring evil spirits back with her. I never told my mother that I was willing to take that chance, that I missed Shimá Sání and still had so much to ask her and learn from her.

Suddenly the morning wind intensified. It was a cold wind now.

I reached for my jacket. As I did, I felt Shimá Sání's corn kernel necklace against my neck. She gave it to me before she left the hogan for the last time. It was all that I had of Shimá Sání, plus the dream catcher and unanswered questions.

Looking down at the necklace, I wondered if Shimá Sání ever thought of coming back to the living, or how she would even do that. Or was she too afraid of the evil spirits to try.

I looked back to the valley.

At first it was a low cloud of dust moving along the desert floor. Then I saw them. Wild dogs. At least a dozen of them.

I reached into the back of the truck.

I thought of my dad. "Shoot them, son."

I steadied my hand and pointed. It was heavy, but I was able to glide it along with the running dogs. It was a skill I developed years ago when hunting with my father.

Then that familiar sound. A loud click. Then more, clicks.

Done, I tossed the camera onto the front seat. Enough photos for today.

Behind me I heard the clap of thunder. A storm was moving in from the west.

Another booming clap of thunder.

I smiled. Grandma would definitely have something to say at this moment.

"First thunder of spring wakes up the rattlesnakes. They'll be leaving their underground hideaways soon," she would warn me whenever we heard the first spring thunder.

My cell phone rang.

"Hi, honey."

It was my wife.

"Will you be home for breakfast?"

"Expect so."

"Billy is looking forward to you taking him fishing."

"On my way."

As I snapped my seatbelt, I took a final look. Far down in the valley I saw the hogan. Not much remained. Weather and time had taken its toll.

But my memories remained. My questions too.

As the truck headed out of the valley, and the East and West Mittens grew smaller in my rear-view mirror, I reached for the dream catcher. Then I started crying. The memories tugged tears from my eyes. I thought of all those unanswered questions.

The ranger station came into view. I stopped the truck at the exit station. The park ranger inside was a young kid, a Navajo. I rolled down my side window.

"Yá'át'ééh," I said.

"What?" was his reply. He was confused.

"Sorry, hello."

"Yeah, hello."

"I'm done with my shift, nothing but a few wild dogs. No trespassers."

"Will you be back tomorrow?"

Just then it started to rain. The red dust was washing off the hood of my ranger's truck. Streaks of red meandered down the windshield.

"Mother-in-law chaser," I said.

"What?"

"Rain. Navajos call rain mother-in-law chasers."

"Okay." His voice had a tone of who cares.

Yes, who cares, I thought. The young Navajo generation. Our culture was slowly disappearing. I wondered what Spider Mother would think.

Would she say that life had become comfortable? Too comfortable, I wondered.

Would she know that I missed my life in the hogan? That I missed all of that and especially, Shimá Sání.

Well, perhaps not all of that. Certainly, I wouldn't miss the return of the rattlesnakes. But then Mother Spider probably knew that too.

WHERE AM I?

I DIDN'T SEE IT COMING.

It had a sting like a bolt of lightning.

I felt the darkness washing over me.

And then nothing.

I shook myself back to consciousness. The first thing noticed was the pain. It was excruciating. My chest was on fire. My head was exploding.

Trying to remember where I was, where I had been. It was all a fog. Nothing was there.

My eyes were puffy, swollen. I tried to open them but couldn't.

Was I dreaming? Had I died? Nothing made sense.

My ears were ringing. A roar, that seemed to be getting louder. That's all I could hear. The damn roar.

Definitely, the taste of blood in my mouth. I ran my tongue over my teeth. Jesus, were those missing teeth?

I wanted to speak, I wanted to scream.

"What the hell is happening. Where the hell am I?"

I heard my voice in my head, but there was no reply. Just the ringing in my ears.

I must be alone. But where am I?

I tried to get up, but I couldn't. I didn't have the strength to even sit up, plus the feeling in my legs was gone. God, was I paralyzed?

Suddenly, I felt the rush of vomit. Up my throat, out my mouth. Acidity vomit, burning my throat, coating my lips. I choked.

Fuck, what's happening to me?

My eyes started to open. Ever so slightly.

Intense lights above me. Blinding me. All I could see were intense white lights.

Then a shadow. Was that a person?

"Please help me."

The shadow came closer. All I could make out was a silhouette against the bright white lights. I tried to focus, but I couldn't.

The dizziness suddenly hit me. The lights were spinning, the silhouette too. I closed my eyes, but the sensation remained. Like spinning in a dark room.

Trying to remember my name. The day? The year? Nothing. It was all a blank. My memory had been erased.

The pain in my chest worsened. It was hard to breathe. I felt I was gasping for air. Air, I needed air.

I was losing it. I felt my body going numb.

Suddenly there was a sharp slap against my face.

I just wanted to slip away. I wanted this to be over.

Another slap, even harder.

Just let me go, I thought. I'm done.

The surface was cold, smooth, but terribly cold. I felt the cold surface against my bare back.

The dizziness worsened. I felt more acidity liquid rising in my throat.

Shaking now. My body was shaking. My arms, my legs, shaking. I couldn't stop them. Jesus, I'm losing control.

My body went limp. The shaking was over. The dizziness lessened.

I opened my eyes again. There were two silhouettes. And they were close.

Then I felt a touch. On my shoulder. Could it be, or am I dreaming?

"Please, help me." This time I heard my voice. Weak, but me. I had spoken. But to whom?

My ears were still ringing. If there was a reply, I couldn't make it out above the roaring in my head.

Then another touch. A hand, perhaps. An open hand, on my head. Rubbing my forehead. So gentle.

There was someone there. I was not alone. I wanted to cry, and I did.

I could feel the tears swelling in my eyes, rolling down my cheekbones, and off my jaw.

"Easy, big guy. We're here." It was a voice. I could hear again. The ringing was gone.

It was then that I knew. I would be alright. A rush of confidence washed over me.

I continued to cry.

Suddenly, I felt myself being raised up to a sitting position.

Trying to focus, I saw flashing lights. So many of them. The dizziness returned.

I closed my eyes and fell back on to the cold surface. Gasping for air.

Something was placed over my mouth and nose. I heard a hissing noise and felt a cool breeze against my face.

"Breathe deeply, slowly. You'll be fine."

That voice again. The same reassuring voice.

Breathing was easy now. My lungs filled with air. I could feel my chest rising and falling. My ribs hurt, but the air felt so good.

I was still in pain. My head was throbbing.

I was sitting up again. The flashing lights were everywhere.

"Can you stand? Do you think you can stand?"

The feeling in my legs had returned.

"Yes, I think so."

I was standing now. My hands were hanging at my side. My eyes were starting to focus.

He was standing next to me. I heard his voice again. I recognized the voice. I knew him.

Then I heard that sound. So many times, I had heard it.

It was coming back now. I recognized where I was.

More flashing lights and then another voice.

"The winner, and still heavy weight champion of the world, by a knockout, Muhammad Ali."

His hand went skyward. Mine stayed at my side.

Then I heard him. "Float like a butterfly, sting like a bee."

More like lightning, I thought.

Jesus, I had just been knocked out by the champ, Muhammad Ali. And it was in the first round. That's all I lasted.

Well, I thought, as my cornerman slipped off my gloves, something to tell my grandkids.

THE PAINTING

"**G**OING ONCE, GOING TWICE, SOLD."

I really didn't want to be here. But she insisted.

"Our next item is an oil painting. Estimated to be about sixty years old. Original frame, original glass and ready to be hung."

I told her auctions were not my thing.

"Oh, come on. It'll be fun."

Not my idea of fun, I told her. But she was relentless.

"Come on. You say we don't do enough together. This will be a chance to do something together."

I wanted to tell her I was thinking of going to a baseball game. Yes, that type of togetherness. That's what I was hoping for. But then I remembered that she didn't like baseball. Jesus how was that possible. Not liking baseball.

"Okay, I'll go, but …"

"But what?"

"We have to go to a baseball game together."

I was sure that would end her push to go to the auction, but,

"Okay, as long as it's not a night game."

And so here I was, on this warm Sunday afternoon, sitting in a large room at this estate auction. Glancing out the window, looking at the tall trees in the distance and the well-kept grounds. Watching people bid on and buy things which will probably end up in their attics, or in their basements.

"Oh, look at that lovely picture. The little girl looks so happy. We need to buy that for our living room."

It was a black and white oil portrait of a little girl. Probably ten years old. Smiling, but also a look of concern, I thought. Concerned about what, I wondered? Curly hair. Big brown eyes focused straight on the viewer. Like she was looking at me. How curious?

"Jesus, I don't know. I mean ..."

Before I could finish, she put up her hand.

"Thirty dollars."

"Thirty dollars to the young lady in the back. Do I hear forty?"

Young lady, Jesus, he called her a young lady. Here we were, she in her seventies and he's calling her a young lady. Oh well, it did bring a smile to her face. Kind of like that oil painting of the little girl.

"Forty." A voice from the other side of the room.

"Forty, do I hear fifty?"

"Fifty," she shouted. She squeezed my hand. Clearly, she wanted this painting.

"Fifty, do I hear sixty?"

The room grew silent. Like a vice, I groaned. My hand was in a vice, aching from her tightening squeeze. Jesus, so strong for her age. I used to be that way. Strong hands, but not now.

"Going once, going twice, sold to the young lady in the back for fifty dollars."

And so, it was ours. For fifty dollars, it was ours. Fifty dollars, for a smile and a glimpse into someone's past. Fifty dollars for memories buried by time. All for fifty dollars.

"I wonder who she is?" She asked the auctioneer as we picked up our prize at the end of the day.

"Story goes that she lived on this estate with her two parents. Their only child. About seventy years ago. Elizabeth was her name. But her story has a tragic ending."

"What was that?"

"She disappeared in the woods surrounding the house and was

never seen again. Some speculated kidnapping, others suggested some wild animals, while some thought it might have been …". He paused, and then changed the subject.

"Look how her eyes seem to follow you when you walk by."

"Interesting," I said as I walked from side to side. Indeed, her eyes are following me. But how does that happen?"

"Well, early Italian painters realized that through the mastery of shadows and lighting, they could create the illusion of depth and distance, thus creating a painting which seemed alive with eyes that were following us."

"Leonardo Da Vinci's Mona Lisa is probably the most famous example of this optical illusion on a two-dimensional surface. Her mysterious eyes seem to be looking directly at you from wherever you're standing."

And with that explanation, we were on our way home with our newly acquired oil painting.

"Do you think it will look good here?" She was holding the painting above the fireplace in the living room.

"Wherever."

And so, the painting of the little girl ended up above the fireplace, above the mantelpiece, observing our every move with those eyes that followed us. Those eyes that concealed a tragic life cut short.

I first noticed the change one morning. That smile, that smile, was not there. Replaced by a sadness, a look of despair.

"Don't you see the change? She's not smiling."

"Sorry, I don't see it. All I see is that little girl smile."

Jesus, I thought, what is happening? Why do I see a sad little girl?

After a while, the sadness changed. Now she appeared to be angry. Whenever I was in the room, her angry eyes followed me.

"Now she's angry. Definitely angry."

"Really, I think you need to take a deep breath. There is no change that I can see."

But the changes continued. One day the little girl's anger was replaced by a look of fear.

"Look now. She's frightened. Can't you see it in her eyes."

"I have no idea what you're talking about, what you see, but I see that same painting, of a smiling, happy girl, that we purchased at the auction."

For weeks I avoided the painting. I went out of my way to avoid it.

Late one night I heard the crash. Glass falling onto the floor. Coming from the living room.

Turning on the light I saw it. The picture was still above the fireplace, but the glass in the picture frame had shattered. Pieces covered the floor.

Moving closer I could see her eyes. They were looking straight at me. And, oh God, she was crying. Tears were running down her face and on to the mantelpiece. Jesus, she was crying.

"What's going on?"

"Come look."

She did.

With the old glass having fallen from the painting, the detail was clearer now.

"Look," she said. "There is a forest in the background. A river too. And ..."

"What?" I replied.

"There's a young boy, standing next to one of the trees."

Indeed, there was. A young boy. He was smiling too.

"Oh my God," she was almost screaming. "That boy, he looks like... you."

"Don't be silly."

"No, no, he does. Your mom showed me pictures of you as a kid. That's you. I'm sure of it."

Of course, she was right. But could I tell her now? The secret behind the little girl's eyes. Was it time to tell her?

"Come sit down. I have something to tell you. Something I should have told someone a long time ago."

I took the picture down and carried it to the couch. She followed me.

"When I was around ten, my dad owned a local lawn service. I would go with him during the summer. One of his customers were the Lloyds. They lived on that estate." I stopped, not sure I wanted to continue.

"Go on."

I cleared my throat.

"Well Elizabeth and I became friends. While my dad was tending to the lawn, Elizabeth and I would play hide and seek in the forest next to the river."

She noticed the tears swelling up in my eyes, but she didn't mention them.

"And?"

"One day we were sitting on a rock overlooking the river, when it happened."

I looked down at the painting in my hands. Elizabeth's tears had stopped, but now mine were falling on the painting. On Elizabeth.

"That day, when we first kissed."

My hands started shaking. The painting almost fell to the floor.

"Her dad saw us. He was very angry. He called her a slut. And then he hit her, hard, and she fell backwards, her head smacked against a large rock."

I was crying. The memories from long ago had resurfaced. No holding back now.

"He made me dig a grave in the basement of the house. That's where we buried her. When I was finished, he told me if I ever told anyone, he would come after me and my parents."

"Well, you must tell someone now."

"Yes, indeed, I will. Elizabeth deserves it. Her secret needs to be told."

I held the painting up in front of me. She had waited sixty years for me to return. Finally, her story would be told.

She was smiling again, and she was happy again, I could see it in her eyes. I was happy too, just like that day we kissed sixty years ago.

THE LAST HARVEST

FROM THE HORIZON TO THE east appeared bands of red and orange, like giant fingers extending upward and outward. Waving at me. The morning sky was on fire. The sun was hiding below the horizon. But not for long.

Suddenly, with the appearance of a bright golden disk, the sun announced its morning arrival. Its reassuring warmth on my weathered face soon followed. Birds took flight. Night crickets fell silent. The colorful fingers vanished, but the warmth remained.

"I like sunrises."

"Sunsets? What about sunsets?"

"Na. Only sunrises."

"Why?"

"Sunrises give me hope. Like I have been born anew."

"And sunsets? What do they give you?"

"Apprehension. Approaching doom."

"Huh."

"But a sunrise, it strips away the cloak of darkness. It chases away the night. It's a new beginning. A chance for a new journey, to change course. To right, wrongs."

We were standing on the deck overlooking the vast farmland to the east. The corn fields were ready for harvest. Silk had risen from the ear shoots about three weeks ago and was just now turning brown.

The female flower was announcing harvest time. Waiting a few more days would be a disaster as the kernels would become hard and starchy. Cattle feed at that point.

"That's why I insisted that the front porch face this way. In the direction of the sunrise."

"Oh."

"Yeah, nothing to the west. Just an ugly barn with one old combine harvester, a couple of rundown tractors, and assorted farming equipment."

Standing next to me, my son, my only son. Towering over me now. He had come to visit. Probably felt guilty for staying away for so long. But then he was working in the big city. A busy guy, I suppose. Career. Schedules. Things he had to do I suppose, like me and my corn in need of harvest.

"How have you been dad?"

"Getting by."

"Well, I've been worried about you, especially since mom …"

He still couldn't bring himself to say it. I looked at him. I wanted to say it was okay.

"I've been fine. Slowing down, but fine. No need to worry yourself."

"Taking your medication?"

"Nah, I stopped. It wasn't doing any good and damn expensive too."

"But doesn't it help you deal with mom's …"

Again, he couldn't say it. Would he ever, I wondered. But then did it really matter?

"Nothing helps with that."

Actually, the medication did help. It relaxed me, took the edge off, but also dulled my memories. Those wonderful memories of Emily were slipping away. That's why I stopped. I didn't want to forget. They were too precious. Perhaps that's all I had left. My memories and my annual corn harvest. And of course, sunrises. That was my life now.

"Would you like another coffee, dad?"

"Sure, but give it two sugars this time."

"Dad, you know what the doctor said. Sugar and your diabetes. Not a good combination."

"Christ son, at my age, what difference does it make? In fact, make it three."

We both broke out in laughter. It felt good. It broke the growing tension between us.

He came over to me. His hands outstretched. We hugged. I felt his scratchy morning beard against my face, but I didn't mind it one bit.

"I love you dad."

I didn't want to let go; I could have held on to him forever.

"I love you too."

We slowly separated. Not because I wanted to, but I could sense he was finished and needed his space. Well, at least I got an I love you.

"Here's your coffee. One sugar."

The sun was high above. Soon on the downside, its day's journey would end behind the hills to the west. And then night.

Why had he come? My son. I hadn't seen him in years. Guilt? Concern? I wondered, but I didn't dare ask. Perhaps if I did, he would leave. And I didn't want that. Not yet anyway.

"How's the combine harvester? I'm surprise you haven't replaced it."

We were in the old barn now. Sun light was raining in through the missing shingles on the roof. There was that smell. Dusty, old wood, rotting corn husks. I loved it. I would miss it, like I missed Emily.

"The combine is fine. Sometimes it balks when I try to start it and occasionally it stops in the middle of the corn field."

The 1972 John Deere 4400 Combine, the King of the Harvest, was parked at the far end of the barn. Like a 5-ton mythical dragon, with an imposing 20-foot front end header, resembling a row of giant, sharp, green teeth, ready to devour five rows of corn with each passing. Sleeping now, but soon it would be awake.

"I guess it's just showing its age like me. But I'm sure it will be okay for the upcoming harvest."

Old like me, I thought. How many years had I been here on this farm, here in Iowa? The farm that was a wedding gift from Emily's parents. God, what did I know about farming back then? Corn was something I bought at the local grocery store.

"If you're a farmer, you'll always have a job," Emily's dad told me. Of course, he was a farmer. Corn too.

But then he didn't tell me about the damaging droughts, and the relentless bugs, the fierce winds, and the long hours. He neglected to tell me about the volatile prices too, and the financial losses I would have to endure. Up before the sun rose. In the fields until dusk. The God damn dirt, the blowing dirt, in my eyes, in my lungs, everywhere. The coughing. Jesus, what a job.

The fact that I wanted to be a professional baseball player was not part of his equation.

"All that time away from your wife" he said. "Be a farmer, you'll have every day with her. You'll grow old together."

But he was wrong, as the blowing dirt and the long tough farming hours took her from me, long before it was her time. And I was left alone with the corn and the annual harvest.

Before Emily took ill, we did enjoy life together on the farm. Raised our only child here in the middle of Iowa. The three of us. After a while I didn't even think about baseball. Just tending to the corn and enjoying my time with the family.

But that changed so quickly. After the harvest in '03. Our son left for college and Emily started coughing. Just occasionally at first, then all the time. It got so bad, she would bend over in pain. Sometimes falling on the floor. And then there was the blood.

Eventually, they ran those terrible tests and they found it.

"I think we should head back to the house, the wind's picking up." My son was at the open barn door. The wind was whipping at his shirt. He was holding on to his hat.

I looked at him and remembered back when he was a young boy. He loved the barn. He would hide in it sometimes, and of course I would pretend I couldn't find him even though he would always be behind the new combine harvester.

"Sure, best we do."

We were sitting at the kitchen table in silence. Probably run out of things to say, things to talk about. There was a slight uneasiness between us, again.

"I better get going. It's a long drive to the airport." He was standing now.

One final hug and off he was. The rental car left a trail of dust as it headed east.

It was 3 o'clock. Still time to tend to the corn.

I walked to the barn. My hips ached. They always did. Swinging open the tall barn doors, I wondered why I didn't get that hip replacement years ago, when the doctors recommended it. Emily wanted me to do so too. Damn, I was too stubborn. A little scared too, but I never told her that.

The combine harvester was facing me. The green dragon was ready to wake from its long rest. Covered in dust and debris from last year's corn harvest. Not sure why I didn't clean it. Perhaps I didn't expect to see another harvest back then.

I fired up the combine. It didn't balk. The dragon was awake and ready to pounce. We slowly crept out of the barn. I smiled. If this were to be my last harvest, I thought, damn it, it would be my best. Emily would be proud.

THE CURSE OF THE COLONEL

IT WAS A PERFECT NIGHT for a baseball game.

The rain which had been in the forecast, stayed away. The wind too, was not a factor, so it didn't favor, or hinder the batters.

On the cool side, but not cold.

Yes, it was a perfect night for a baseball game.

It was the bottom of the 12th inning, and the score was tied at 3.

The home team was batting.

With two outs, the batter hit a lazy fly ball to the outfield.

It was an easy out to end the inning.

As the visiting team ran off the field and into the dugout, I noticed that they continued to run into the tunnel leading to their locker room.

The home team was nowhere to be seen. They didn't take the field for the next inning.

"Hey, what's going on?" I asked.

"What do you mean?"

"Where are the teams?"

"Huh?"

"It's the thirteenth inning. Where are the teams?"

"The game is tied."

"Yes, I know, so where are the teams? Where did they go?"

"But, the game is over. What would you expect the teams to do?"

"What? How can the game be over. It's 3 all."

As I looked around, I noticed the fans were leaving the stadium. Like the ball players they were heading for the exits.

I was confused, so I turned to Alex for an explanation.

"People are leaving. What the hell is going on?"

"The game was tied at the end of the 12th inning. Simple as that."

"No, it's not simple. I'm confused."

Alex looked at me like he couldn't understand why I was confused.

The Giants had come to town. The Tokyo Giants. And they were playing our team, the Hanshin Tigers, Osaka's team.

The Hanshin Tigers, whose most memorable night occurred in 1985 when they won the Japanese World Series. It was the first time they had won the World Series.

Fans had waited so long for a championship that they lost themselves in the excitement of the moment.

Leaving the stadium, they came across a Kentucky Fried Chicken. The tall statue of Colonel Sanders reminded them of the hero of the series, an American player by the name of Randy Bass.

In a burst of wild jubilation and without giving it a second thought, the fans removed the Colonel, carried him to the Dotonbori River, and tossed him into the muddy water, where he abruptly sank to the bottom.

And so, on that night, the curse of the Colonel began.

In all the years that followed the Tigers didn't make it back to the World Series. In fact, they never even came close. For the next 18 seasons the Tigers lost more games than they won. The Colonel at the bottom of the Dotonbori River saw to that.

Realizing their terrible mistake, a call to raise the Colonel out of the Dotonbori River commenced. But first they had to find him. Divers began searching at the bottom of the river.

Finally in March of 2009, the water-soaked Colonel was lifted from the river, but time had taken its toll on him. The Colonel was missing his left hand and his eyeglasses.

In an attempt to placate the Colonel's spirit, his plastic body was placed at a KFC close to the Tiger's ballpark. Every Tiger fan assumed the curse would be lifted.

"I still don't understand what's happening here," I said turning back to Alex.

"The game is over. That's all."

"Yes, but it was a tie."

"Yes, after 12 innings. Game over."

"But back home, they'd play until one team wins."

"Really?"

"I once went to a game that lasted 22 innings. The Colorado Rockies scored a run in that inning to beat the San Diego Padres. Hell of a game."

"How long?"

"What?"

"How long did the game last?

"Over six hours."

Alex just shook his head.

"And I stayed for the whole game. Most fans did too."

"Why?"

"Because a tie game is like kissing your sister."

"I don't understand."

"Because it is."

"No, no, I mean why would anyone want to kiss his sister?"

"Just an expression, Alex, just an expression."

"Yeah, what's with those? You Americans are full of them."

"But they are very useful."

"Sure, like behind the eight ball, or shooting the breeze."

"Okay, perhaps they're not the best examples."

The stadium was nearly empty now. The dirt in the infield was being raked for tomorrow's game.

"So, Alex, are they going to continue this game tomorrow?"

"No, the game is over. It's a tie. It counts as a tie game in the standings. New game tomorrow."

"But why did it end after 12 innings?"

"Oh, that's easy. That's so the fans can catch the last train home."

"Huh?"

"And by the way, while we've been shooting the breeze, the last train left the station."

We both started laughing even though it was going to cost a fortune to take a taxi home.

Exiting the stadium, I glanced over at the Dotonbori River. I tried to imagine what that night in 1985 was like when the Colonel was tossed from the Ebisu Bridge.

"I have a question, Alex."

"Yes."

"The curse. Did it end when the Colonel was returned to dry land?"

Looking at me, a big smile came over Alex's face.

"Well let me put it this way Michael. The Hanshin Tigers are still trying to move from behind that eight ball."

LESSON LEARNED

"GO AHEAD TAKE IT."

They already had. I hesitated.

"Hurry, before he gets back."

I looked outside. He had just finished pumping the gas and was checking the oil.

"What are you waiting for?"

"I'm not sure we should be doing this."

"Come on, everybody does it."

The hood of the car slammed shut. It was a brand new '49 Chevrolet. Red and white. Must be someone passing by. No one here owns a cool car like that. The doctor in town could, but he'd rather drive that old junker. Most people around here did.

"He's coming this way. Do it now."

They had already snatched their favorite candy bar from the display on the counter.

A Baby Ruth. That was my favorite. They must have named it after the Babe, my hero. Thank goodness Boston traded him to the Yankees. He was the best, just like the candy bar I was shoving in my front pocket.

The front door swung open, just as I pulled my shirt out to cover the incriminating bulge in my pant pocket.

"Hey boys, can I help you? Need something?"

It was Mister Killian. He owned the only gas station in town. It was a Texaco station. Its pole with the big red star atop stood taller than anything in town and could be seen far before entering town. Mister Killian was so proud of that sign. "This is the future of advertising," he would tell us.

Then he would talk about the gasoline he sold. "Sky Chief, the best gasoline money could buy. 27 cents a gallon, up from 24 cents two years ago, but still a great gasoline." He couldn't tell us enough about gasoline.

It was 1949. The town we lived in "had more dogs than people," my dad would say. I never counted either, but I was sure he was right.

Upstate New York, off the beaten path. "People only stop here for gasoline, or directions," my mother would say. "Certainly not to eat, 'cause we have no restaurants, unless you count the candy display at old Killian's gas station."

The candy display. Almond Joy, Bazooka Bubble Gum, Junior Mints, Dots Gum Drops, World's Candy Cigarettes, and of course, Baby Ruth.

Mister Killian was walking with a limp now. Damn arthritis, he would complain. Then he would smile and say, "you know Arthur Itis, husband of Mary Itis."

Killian had been a fixture in our community as far back as anyone could remember. We all loved him. Rumor had it he once had a wife, but she left him for the big city. With no children of his own, he kind of adopted all the young children in town, and that included me.

For hours I would sit in his garage while he worked on cars.

"Changing oil and changing tires, I'm always changing things," he would say. Sometimes he would let me put air in the new tires. I loved the whooshing sound of the air and the smell of the new tires.

"Someday, I will be a gas station man," I would tell Mister Killian.

He would always reply, "stay here long enough, and you can have this one."

"So, do you boys need anything today?" He repeated.

I was too busy worrying about the Baby Ruth in my pocket to reply. Neither did Tommy or Bobby.

"Cats got your tongues?"

Finally, I spoke for the three of us.

"Oh no, Mister Killian, we just came in to get out of the sun and to see you."

He was looking at us, the kind of look you see when someone doesn't quite believe what he's seen, or heard. Then he looked at the candy display. And back to us. Oh God, did he notice three were missing.

"You want to buy some candy today?" He asked.

We three shook our heads no.

"Or a soda, perhaps?"

"Not today, Mister Killian, I said as I was moving towards the front door. "Too close to dinner."

"Of course," he said. "Can't ruin your moms' lovely dinner."

Without saying goodbye, we left.

"Do you think he suspected something?" Tommy asked.

"Not sure, but he was looking at the candy display for a long time," I replied. "What do you think Bobby?"

"Christ, who cares. It was only a nickel. He only lost a nickel from each of us."

"But do you think he noticed?"

"You two can worry about that. I'm going to eat my candy bar. And the next time, I might take two. Maybe three."

"But Bobby, it's Mister Killian."

"So what? What's he ever done for us?"

What's he done, Mister Killian? I didn't know about Tommy or Bobby, but I knew. All those hours, in his shop, like a grandfather to me. Occasionally giving me a cola from the soda machine. Letting me sit in the front seat of the cars he was working on. Pretending I was driving the country roads around our town. Showing me how to read an oil gauge. How to clean a spark plug. And on special occasions, letting me pour the oil into the engine. Jesus, what did he do for me? I certainly knew.

I was back in my bedroom after dinner. "Take a shower tonight," mom told me."

As the warm water rain down my face, I couldn't tell. I couldn't tell which was the shower and which were the tears. I can't believe I did that, took that Baby Ruth. And didn't pay. That was… stealing, I thought.

Out of the shower and into my bedroom.

There was mom, she did not look happy. Then I saw what she was holding. The Baby Ruth. I forgot to take the candy bar out of my pocket.

"Care to explain this?" She said, "I know you didn't have any money today."

I stood there in my New York Yankees pajamas. If only I could lose myself in the pin stripes.

"I'm waiting, young man."

That was a definite sign that I was in trouble. Young man was a dead giveaway. I could certainly expect a spanking after this.

"They dared me to."

"Dared you to do what exactly."

Oh God, she wants details. Yes, I'm in big trouble. Really big.

"To take a candy bar."

"And how did you pay for this candy bar, young man."

There it was again. Twice. This will not end well I thought. And wait until dad gets involved.

"Didn't."

"You didn't pay for the candy bar. You stole the candy bar?"

Jesus, was I a thief, a common criminal? Would I go to jail, like Uncle Fred did when he stole that car? I started crying. Shaking. Waiting for my punishment to begin. Waiting for the first hit.

It never came.

"I want you to get in bed, with your stolen candy bar and think about what you've done and what you're going to do."

She turned off the light and closed the door. "That's it?" I whispered. "That's it?"

The next morning, when I came to the breakfast table, they were there. My dad was finishing his coffee and getting ready to leave for work.

"I have to leave a little early today. Need to put gas in the car and of course spend a few minutes with Mister Killian. I haven't seen him for a while. Have you?"

Dad was looking directly at me. "Have you?"

"Yesterday, on the way home from playing baseball."

"That's nice. How's he doing?"

"Alright, I guess."

He got up, kissed me on the head, and reached for his car keys.

"Quite a guy, Mister Killian, quite a guy. He'll sure be missed when …"

My dad stopped before finishing. My mom was shaking her head. The front door closed. We heard the car start.

"What was dad going to say?" I asked.

"Oh nothing. Just finish your breakfast and get on with your day."

But I couldn't finish my breakfast. I just stared at the almost full bowl of Rice Krispies. Soggy now, and no more snap, crackle, or pop.

Watching my spoon slip beneath the cereal, I looked up at mom.

"Could I have an advance on my allowance?" I asked.

"How much?"

"Ten cents will do."

Reaching in her purse, she pulled at a shiny dime. "I have no nickels, is a dime ok?"

"Sure, that'll work."

I excused myself from the breakfast table and ran all the way to the gas station. No one was at the pump. The front door was closed, locked. There was a sign on the door. Closed until further notice.

I noticed the garage door was open. I ducked my head and walked inside.

He was there. Changing a tire. He looked so tired.

"Mister Killian, it's me Michael. How come the station's closed?"

"No gas, Texaco ran out of gas."

"I'm sorry."

"No matter, hardly anyone stops here anymore, with that new highway across the way."

There was a sadness in his voice. He struggled to get up.

"Arthur Itis?" I asked.

"Yea, him and Mary, today. Both of them." He was laughing now, then he started coughing.

"What are you doing here this morning, Michael. I figured you'd be playing baseball with your friends."

My friends, I thought. Not sure about them. Not sure after yesterday.,

"Not today. No baseball today."

"So, what can I do for you?"

I stood there, trying to find the right words. Could there ever be right words, I wondered.

I slowly removed the candy bar out of my pocket. It was soft from the heat of my body.

"A Baby Ruth. Isn't that your favorite?"

"I'm sorry," I said.

"For what?"

"For taking this yesterday?"

"Oh, did you forget to pay?"

He was giving me an out. That's what Mister Killian was doing. I could have said yes, and that would have ended it. But I couldn't.

"No, I didn't forget."

"Oh."

He knew exactly what I was trying to say, without saying it. I could just tell.

"Here is ten cents for that candy bar." I was holding out the shiny dine.

He took it and put his hand on my shoulder.

"I think I owe you some change, but the office is closed," he said.

"I do have some extra soda over here. New ones too. Doctor Pepper. How would you like one of those? I suspect, if you're going to help me change the oil in this car, you might get thirsty."

The rest of that day was one of the best days of my life. Mister Killian actually let me change a spark plug. Not only did I learn how to change a spark plug, but I also learned a valuable lesson thanks to my mom.

Years have gone by. We moved from that small town in upstate New York to California. I still have an occasional Baby Ruth and when I do, I always think of him, Mister Killian, the oil gauge, the tires, and of course changing that spark plug.

THE SACRED CENOTE
OF CHICHEN ITZA

THE SMOOTH PAVEMENT WAS HOURS behind us. It was all dirt now. And ruts, big ones too. Dust everywhere. Dry as a bone. Hot. Too damn hot.

But the four-wheel drive Jeep was right at home.

We hadn't seen anyone for quite some time, not that we were surprised. Who else would want to be out here, in the jungle? With two crazy Americans?

We left Merida about four hours ago, after a night in the old Merida Hotel. Just a short distance from the dock where we disembarked after an overnight journey on a small freighter from Vera Cruz. Sleeping outside on the narrow deck, watching the stars move up and down along with the horizon. The sea was rough that night and the ship was at its mercy. We were too, after that spicy pre-boarding meal and those tequila shots.

Cheaper than flying and quicker than driving, Stewart said, so we boarded this dilapidated freighter as the sun was setting and headed south to Merida, on the coast of the Yucatán Peninsula.

We were in search of the sacred pools of Yucatán. Deep pools in the dense jungle, where ancient Mayans were supposed to have worshiped underwater gods. As part of their ceremony, they sacrificed young maidens to these gods by tossing them over the cliffs into the dark pools below. Gold too, that was part of the ceremony to appease the gods.

The jeep hit a big pothole, and the diving gear in the back clanged together. The gear that we rented at the dive shop in Merida.

"This stuff looks kinda old and worn," Stewart noted.

"No senor, this is top of the line. The best." the owner of the dive shop replied in broken English.

"If this is the best, I'd like to see his worst," I replied. Stewart just grinned. The owner frowned.

"Oh, we'll also need a rope ladder. About 100 feet."

"Si senor. Nueva o vieja?"

"New."

The jungle was denser now, overgrown with trees and tangled vegetation. The ground thick with vines, and shrubbery, and of course insects. The insects were everywhere. Relentless insects. The trees were blocking out the sun. The temperature was falling.

Sacred Mayan pools were scattered throughout the Yucatán Peninsula in southern Mexico. Called "cenote" by the Mayans, they were formed when the roof of an underground cavern collapsed revealing a deep water filled sinkhole. These sinkholes were revered by the Mayans as the entrance to the underworld and the residency of mysterious gods.

The Mayans, of 2,000 years ago, who built the impressive pyramids throughout the Yucatán Peninsula. The Mayans whose civilization stretched through Central America, held one cenote especially sacred, the massive Cenote of Chichen Itza. Worshippers from all over the region would travel to this most sacred cenote with offerings to the god Chaac, the rain god, who lived at the bottom of this deep, dark sinkhole.

Chaac was feared by the Mayans because they believed he held the power of drought, or life sustaining rain over them. Through their offerings they hoped to receive abundant rains and good harvests.

"What do you need the rope ladder for?" He was holding the rope in his hands and looking right at me. He approached me, waiting for an answer. I hesitated.

When I first entered his dive shop, I noticed the dark skin, dark eyes, and straight black hair. But now standing directly in front of me I was drawn to other characteristics. Barely 5 feet tall, a perfectly shaped Roman nose, the extra fold in his eyelids, and his long sloping forehead. The colorful stone inlays which had been placed in his front teeth.

He was Mayan. One of the 1.5 million Mexicans who could trace their lineage back to the Golden Age of the Mayan Empire. All that was missing was a large, colorful headdress, the distinguishing mark of a Mayan ruler.

"We normally hang the rope ladder off the side of our boat and use it when we're ready to get out of the water."

"So, you're headed out to the ocean?"

"Yes, of course, what did you think?"

He didn't answer. But he looked at me like he didn't believe me. He was suspicious.

"Come on Stewart, time to head to the boat."

The Jeep hit another large pothole. The frame scraped the surface. The can of beer I was holding flew from my hand and landed on the dirty floorboard.

"So much for the shocks on this thing," I said.

Stewart was driving, he shrugged.

I wondered if he did it on purpose. Hitting the potholes. It would be just like him. I chuckled, yes, he probably did.

The dirt road came to an end. A locked gate was in front of us. The large sign, in both Spanish and English read,

No Trespassing. Keep Out

We jumped out of the Jeep. We had arrived.

That's when I noticed. The dense jungle smell, the combined scent of vegetation, moisture, soil, and decaying plants and wood. A pleasant smell actually, the smell of life.

Carrying our diving gear, climbing over the locked gate, we made our way in the direction of the Sacred Pool. A beaten path showed the way. Clearly, we were not the first to come here.

After a short walk, we came across a clearing in the jungle. There in the middle of the clearing was the Sacred Cenote of Chichen Itza.

"At the mouth of the well of the Itza," Stewart said as we approached.

"Huh?"

"The translation of Chichen Itza. At the mouth of the well of the Itza."

That was Stewart. A wealth of knowledge. I just mumbled, "Itza. What does that mean?"

"The Itza were the people who inhabited the Yucatán Peninsula during the Golden Age."

"Jesus, how do you know all this stuff?"

Stewart didn't answer. He didn't have too. He was the smart one.

In front of us was a sunken pond, about 200 feet in diameter, about 90 feet below the surface, with limestone walls too steep and too smooth to climb. Overlooking the sinkhole was a small stone platform on two levels. Probably a viewing place from where the Mayan chief could view the ceremony and direct the sacrifices.

Off to one side was another sign, attached to a tree, with large letters. It was faded, but still legible.

Do Not Attempt to Enter the SACRED Pool

And underneath that, someone had written a more ominous warning:

If you do, there is no way out. RIP

"I guess the ancient Mayans didn't have rope ladders," I said. My nervous laugh breaking the silence of the moment. Stewart just looked at me.

Putting on our diving gear and tying one end of the rope ladder to a tree overlooking the sinkhole, we were ready.

"After you." Stewart tossed the rope ladder over the edge and motioned for me to go first.

"Okay, into the mouth of the whatever."

The climb down was difficult. I wondered what the ascent would be like.

My feet reached the surface of the water. I was surprised at how cool it was. I was also surprised at how dark it was.

Stewart soon joined me.

"77 degrees." He said as he entered the water.

"What?"

"The temperature of the water. A constant 77 degrees."

"I'm surprised you didn't give it to me in centigrade."

"Between 24 and 25."

"But, of course."

Adjusting our breathing regulators and securing our masks, we were ready to dive. I gave Stewart a thumbs up and he did the same.

As we descended into the cenote it became more difficult to see. I turned on my diving light, but it's beam hardly penetrated the darkness.

But, we continued downward, into the darkness, into the sacred cenote.

Suddenly, Stewart grabbed my arm and pointed off to my right.

In the darkness I could see what appeared to be two large eyes and an enormous mouth. Teeth too.

I recoiled.

Not wanted to go any deeper, I turned and made my way to the surface. Stewart followed.

"What the hell was that?" I asked as we broke the surface.

"Not sure, but I doubt it's the god Chaac. Shall we go back, and see?"

I reached for the rope ladder. I was ready to climb out of the cenote. Stewart grabbed my arm.

"Come on, one more dive and we'll head back."

"Oh?"

"Yes, let's see what that thing is."

I wanted to say I was finished, finished diving in this sacred cenote, that I wanted to climb back up and head back to our small room at the Merida Hotel. But I didn't.

"Okay, one more dive. Just one."

Back down we dove. Diving lights showing the way. Deeper and deeper, into the mouth of the well of the Itza. Back hundreds of years, into the Sacred Cenote of Chichen Itza.

Then we were there, face to face with it. The two eyes, headlights. The large mouth, an open hood.

It was the front end of a Jeep. A damn Jeep in the sacred cenote.

I pointed upward. I was ready to be done with this dive. Stewart shook his head in agreement.

We broke the surface at the same time. Removing the air regulator from my mouth, I turned to Stewart.

"Jesus, it was a Jeep."

We both started laughing and slapping the water.

Suddenly the rope ladder hit me on my head. As it unraveled from the top of the sinkhole, it slowly covered the entire surface of the water. Like a large snake, coiling in the water. Except it wasn't a snake. It was our ladder.

"What the hell? How did the ladder disconnect from the tree?"

We both looked up. Standing on the edge. It was him. The dive shop owner.

"Thank god, it's you," I shouted. "Can you help us? Throw down a rope ladder so we can climb out of this."

He disappeared.

"Perhaps he's getting a rope ladder."

"Yes, I'm sure."

After a few minutes he returned.

"Jesus, what is that?"

"A headdress, he's wearing a Mayan headdress," I replied. "Worn by the chief."

Then it appeared, the front end of our Jeep.

"What the hell?"

Before I could speak, the Jeep skidded off the top of the cenote and crashed down into the water, just missing us.

As it sank to the bottom, I looked back up. He was gone.

The storm clouds formed in the sky above. Then I heard thunder. As it started to rain, I thought of Chaac. At least it would be a good harvest.

MICHAEL THE …

"**H**E'S MINE?" I ASKED NOT really believing what I was looking at.

"Yes," my mother replied.

My heart was racing with excitement. My emotions swung from wanting to cry to wanting to laugh.

"Really? Mine?"

"Yes, son." It was my dad. The grin on his face reassured me it was true.

Reaching down, looking into his eyes, I felt a joy like none before. A companion, I thought, but not yet realizing he was much more.

His eyes stared back. Wide open, so innocent, almost begging, grabbing me, pulling me in. I was captured.

Mostly black with random patches of white.

Do I dare touch him?

"Go ahead," my mom said, noticing my hesitation.

I offered the back of my hand.

His dark nose rubbed up against my outstretched hand. It was cold, and slightly moist. Rough and crusty too. It tickled me.

Suddenly his dark pink tongue lapped my hand. It was smooth and warm.

We were connecting. Bonding.

His short black tail rose up. It started wagging, slowly at first, then so quickly that I thought he was going to fall over.

"He's happy," I said.

"Yes, he's telling you he's happy to meet you," my mom replied.

And so, it began. My life with my first dog. Although I didn't know it at the time, my life would change in ways I couldn't imagine.

"What name would you like to give your dog?" It was my dad. His hand was resting on my shoulder.

"Can I give it any name?" I replied.

"Of course, Michael, it's your dog."

My dog. Yes, my dog.

He was so small. Just a little dog. No particular breed. Just a mutt, but he was mine. And I was his.

"Michael," I said.

"What?" Both my mom and dad responded at the same time.

"Michael. My dog. I want to call him Michael."

"But ..."

"Michael. That's his name."

"Okay. Michael it is."

From that moment on, there were two Michael's residing in our house, in the countryside, in upstate New York.

I was 6 years old when Michael came into my life. Little did I know at the time about taking care of a pet, let alone a dog.

My naivety was exposed the very first morning when I woke up, jumped out of bed expecting to find Michael, only to land in a warm sticky liquid. Welcome to the responsibility of having a dog, I thought, as I washed Michael's pee from the bottom of my feet. It would be the first of many such learning encounters.

Living in a small town, some called it a village, where there were only a couple of kids my age, Michael quickly became my best friend. We were inseparable.

Of course, there were initial problems for my parents, but their creativity prevailed. When my mom needed one of us, she would get our attention by calling to either "Michael the Boy", or "Michael the Dog."

And so it was, every late afternoon from the open kitchen window I would hear, "Michael the Boy, it's dinner." Of course, both Michaels would rush to the dinner table. Indeed, we were inseparable.

Michael and I loved to go to the nearby pond during the summer. I would fish and he would bark at the flapping trout as I pulled them to the shore. I thought it was his way of saying, "good job, Michael."

In the fall, when I would rake the fallen leaves, Michael would be at my side, snapping at the rake. Then, when I would form a big pile of leaves, he would race through it, spreading my work throughout the yard. It was great fun for him, so I didn't much mind it.

In the winter we played in the deep snow and occasionally we ventured onto the frozen pond. Michael loved the snow, but he wasn't too fond of the frozen pond.

The spring was one of our favorite times. We would go together into the woods and look for baby rabbits. Once we came across a deer with its young. Michael and I would remain still and quiet whenever we came across these animals, with the one exception when he ran after a porcupine. Of course, he only did that once.

As the vet pulled the quills from Michael's face, I looked at my best friend and wondered, "were you trying to protect me from that dangerous looking animal?" I concluded he was because that's what best friends do.

The seasons rushed by, but we never grew tired of one another. Michael the Boy and Michael the Dog were inseparable. He would sleep at the side of my bed and sometimes he would jump up onto the bed and put his face next to mine. I never tired of his cold nose rubbing up against me, or that warm wet tongue, and he never tired of my petting.

When we went for a ride in dad's new Oldsmobile, Michael and I would always sit together in the back. With the window open, he would sniff the air as it rushed by, blowing his hair straight back. I would always hold on to him, fearing he would jump from the speeding car. Of course, he never did. But I wasn't taking any chances with my best friend.

One day, Michael got sick. He was throwing up.

Back to the vet we went.

"Is Michael going to be okay?" I asked as we drove down route 82.

"I'm sure, Michael," my mother said. "The vet will take care of him."

I must have asked dozens of times. Each time mom replied the vet will take care of him. Something in her voice didn't comfort me. But I kept asking.

As we drove to the vet's office, I experienced an overwhelming feeling of loss. I remembered when a distant uncle died a few years back, but I didn't feel anything like now. The possibility of losing Michael was unbearable. I couldn't imagine my life without him.

I was holding him in my crossed arms when we walked into the office. His sad eyes looking up at me. I looked away as tears formed in my eyes.

"Worms," the vet said. "He has worms."

"Worms?" I asked, visualizing the large night crawlers I used to catch fish.

"Very small worms, probably from contact with an infected animal."

I immediately thought of that dead field mouse that Michael was carrying around in his mouth. A week ago, during one of our trips into the woods. I just thought it was funny at the time, but now I realized I should have taken it away. I failed my best friend.

"Will he be okay?" My voice revealed my concern and probably my guilt too.

"Oh yes, it's just worms. We have medication for that. He'll be fine."

And he was. After a week, we were back at the pond. I was fishing, and Michael was exploring and racing to the shore whenever I caught a fish.

The years passed. I was now ten.

It was an early fall morning. Overcast. An earlier drizzle covered the ground. There was a slight chill in the air.

Mom called for me. "Michael the Boy, breakfast is ready."

I ran from the open field, across the road and into the house.

"Where's Michael the Dog," my dad asked.

I looked around. Strange, he didn't follow me.

"I guess he's exploring. Must have discovered something in the open field," I said, hoping it wasn't another dead field mouse.

As I reached for the glass of orange juice, I heard the screech. Loud. Squealing tires on the wet road.

"Oh my God," my mom shouted. She was looking out the kitchen window.

"What mom? What happened?"

She turned away from the window. All the color had drained from her face. She stood there, like she was frozen, with her hand over her mouth. Widening eyes.

Dad rush over to her and caught her as she started to fall.

I ran to the window.

The car had come to a stop in the middle of the road, skid marks appeared on the wet surface. The driver's side door was open. He was kneeling beside his car. Holding something in his hands.

It was Michael the Dog.

The Oldsmobile raced down the road. I had never seen my dad drive so fast.

I was holding Michael in my arms. His eyes looked up at me. I didn't turn away.

His nose rubbed against my bare arm. His cold nose. I thought back to the first day.

I rubbed behind his ears. His tail started wagging.

"You'll be fine," I whispered. "You have to be, you're my best friend."

The vet was waiting for us. Mom had called.

He was on the examination table. His black and white hair matted from the morning drizzle.

The vet was speaking to my dad. I couldn't make out what he was saying.

My dad came over to me and put his hands on my shoulder.

"We should go, Michael. Let the vet do his work."

I saw the tears in his eyes. My dad was crying.

"I want to stay here."

"Are you sure, Michael?"

"Yes, I have to stay."

I felt the tears welling up in my eyes. I heard them hit the examination table. A soft sound. Some landed on Michael.

His tail started wagging. Was he telling me not to be sad? That it was okay?

I looked out the window. It was still overcast. Gray clouds. The drizzle had returned. But it was harder now. The pinging sound against the window almost concealed my soft sobs. Almost.

I put my hand on Michael's head. I wanted to remember this moment. This day.

This day that Michael the Dog, my best friend died. The day when part of Michael the Boy died too.

THE LONG JOURNEY HOME

THE SHINKANSEN PULLED INTO THE station. Japan's bullet train. The sleek white and blue Nozomi was on time to the second. As always.

"You can set your watch to the arrival and departure of the Shinkansen," my co-worker told me. I used to think that he was just trying to impress me as he was Japanese, but I quickly learned he was absolutely correct. I could set my watch to the bullet trains.

The doors opened and arriving passengers stepped onto the platform, heading to the exits.

Those of us, waiting to board, stood in a single line waiting patiently until it was our time. We waited until everyone who wanted to get off the train did. There was no shoving or pushing and certainly no cutting in line. The queue was acknowledged and respected, almost sacred here on the platform, as it was throughout Japan.

As I moved to my seat, I thought about how closely the Shinkansen mirrored Japanese society in general.

On time. Punctual. That was important here in Japan. In fact, even being slightly early for a meeting at my office was seen as being on time. Respecting co-workers, and of course, the boss.

I was ten minutes late for a meeting once because the bus I was on had engine troubles. I could tell when I arrived at the meeting that I had broken an unwritten rule, one of Japan's coveted expectations, I was late. The silent frown from the boss and the sympathetic looks from my co-workers told me everything I needed to know. Of course, no one said anything, because I was a foreigner, a Gaijin.

Being a foreigner in a structured, rules country like Japan is definitely a benefit. Generally, you will be excused or forgiven if you cross the line, if you stumble.

The Nozomi pulled out of the station, accelerating southwest out of Tokyo.

The tall buildings of the capital city were almost a blur at 186 miles per hour. Soon we were out in the countryside. Mountains to the west, the Pacific Ocean to the east.

The ride was surprisingly smooth, and it presented no difficulty to the consumption of my bento lunch of rice and smoked salmon, which I had purchased at the station. Of course, my ability to use the enclosed chopsticks, was another story. But it was either that or eat with my hands. Next time, I'll bring a fork from my apartment.

Even the coffee in my cardboard cup stayed put. Starbucks.

Starbucks had entered the Japanese market a few years ago and had taken the country by storm, especially among young coffee drinkers and those in search of a non-smoking environment in which to enjoy their Pumpkin Spice Latte, or a less exotic, simple Caffe Americano. Since I was a non-smoker, Starbucks was my preferred coffee stop.

Smoking was a real problem in Japan and actually in most of Asia. Japan was behind the U.S. in encouraging or requiring businesses to prohibit smoking. But at least the Shinkansen was non-smoking.

The Shinkansen slowed as we came to our first stop, Yokohama. A few passages got up and moved to the exit. After they exited onto the platform, new passengers entered.

He was an older gentleman; I would guess in his 90s. Slowed by age and walking with a cane. Impeccably dressed. Dark black suit.

He was looking at his ticket, but I could tell he was having trouble reading the small print.

"Sumimasen," he said as he reached out towards me, ticket in hand.

Sumimasen was one of the first Japanese words I learned. Sumimasen, excuse me. A very useful word in so many settings, especially when one wants to apologize in advance for being a burden to someone, like calling for a waitress in a busy restaurant, or asking someone to read their train ticket.

Back home, an apology conveys a feeling of regret, but here in Japan, an apology is seen as an acknowledgment of responsibility and one's humility. As such, it is highly valued by the Japanese.

"Daijobu desu yo," I replied acknowledging his request, "it is fine."

As I took the ticket from his hand, he bowed slightly. "Arigato, thank you," he replied.

"Do you speak English?" I asked.

"Yes, a little. Just a little."

Looking at his ticket, I saw that his seat was the one I was occupying. I was supposed to have been in the aisle seat. Now it was my turn to apologize.

"Sumimasen, I am in your seat. Mine is the one next to it."

I started to get up when he motioned for me to stay seated. "That is okay, I will sit here. And it will be easier with my cane."

Interesting, I thought. He acknowledged my apology by suggesting he would prefer the aisle seat. It was his way of letting me save face, so typical of the Japanese.

"Are you on vacation?" I asked, then realizing what a stupid question that was.

He turned and looked at me. He was taken aback by my question. His face revealed both surprise and slight annoyance. He pointed to his cane.

"No." No was all he said.

Trying to make up for my apparent blunder, I tried a different approach. "Visiting someone?"

"In a way."

He unbuttoned his suit jacket and then I noticed, he was wearing a black tie.

"Oh, I'm sorry."

"That's okay, why should you know." He removed a handkerchief from his shirt pocket and caught a single tear which was moving down his cheek.

The black tie, I should have noticed earlier. In Japan, black ties for funerals, white ties for marriages.

I didn't know what to say. How to continue the conversation. Best to say nothing I thought.

Then it came into view, off to the west. Mount Fuji. Japan's most sacred mountain. with its symmetrical snow-capped cone, the tallest mountain in Japan and long seen as the symbol of the country.

"Utsukushii," he said, pointing to the window. "Beautiful."

"Hai, yes, it is beautiful, and it is especially clear this morning."

"I have climbed that, many times," he said. "Of course, not recently." He let out a slight chuckle and smiled. I assumed we were on good terms again, or at least speaking terms.

"I never have, but perhaps I should."

"Yes, at least once, to touch heaven, a pilgrimage to purify your soul."

As Mount Fuji disappeared behind the speeding Shinkansen, we entered a long tunnel, one of many tunnels that allowed the bullet train to navigate its journey without climbing mountains. Tunnels that leveled the route so that the Shinkansen could maintain a steady speed worthy of a bullet train.

As we exited the tunnel, he tapped me on the shoulder. "And you?"

"Me?"

"Yes, are you visiting?"

"No. My journey is work related."

"Japanese company?"

"No, a foreign company."

"American?"

"Yes, an American company."

He grew silent again and his expression turned to disappointment, almost sad. Again, I was at a loss. I didn't understand what was going on. I didn't know how to ask.

The Shinkansen pulled into the Osaka station. Most of the passengers departed and only a few boarded.

"Is this your destination?" I asked, hoping to restore our relationship.

"No. I am going to the end, the final stop."

"Me too," I replied.

"Yes, it is a long journey today."

That's when I realized he didn't bring a suitcase with him when he boarded. All he had was his cane. Strange, I thought, for someone visiting.

"You certainly travel light," I said, pointing to his cane.

"Oh, yes, but I'm going home."

"Oh, I thought you were visiting someone."

"Yes, that too."

Okay, now I was really confused, but I assumed it was because I was talking to him in English. Of course, I had to, as my Japanese was not that good. Perhaps in time it would be, but not yet.

"American?" He suddenly asked.

"What?"

"Are you an American?"

"Huh, yes."

"From where?"

"Colorado."

"Oh yes, the Rock Mountains."

"Rocky Mountains."

"Oh, Rocky Mountain. Are they sacred?"

"I don't think so."

"Too bad."

The Shinkansen raced to the west now. Our car was almost empty. One more stop before our destination, and my afternoon meeting.

The Shinkansen slowed as we pulled to Kobe Station. The doors opened and many passengers boarded. Mostly older passengers. The car was practically full now.

There was something strange about the new passengers, but I couldn't quite determine what it was. I decided it was best not to stare.

As the Shinkansen left the station for our final stop, I turned to the old man.

"And you, where are you from?"

"Tokyo."

I was taken aback. Tokyo.

"But I thought you were going home. We left Tokyo this morning."

"Yes." That's all he said as he reached in his coat pocket and pulled out his ojuzu. A Japanese prayer bead bracelet.

"Tokyo's my home now, but it wasn't then." he continued. But I was still confused.

As he struggled to put the ojuzu on his wrist, it slipped out of his hands and fell to the floor.

He bent down to retrieve the ojuzu and then I saw it. On the back of his neck. A wide deep scar, covering his neck. A scar, which probably didn't end with the white collar of his shirt.

As he rose back up, he looked at me. He could tell I had noticed the scar. He was not embarrassed, although I certainly was.

"Hibakusha," he said softly.

"What?"

"Hibakusha. Atomic bomb survivor."

"You?"

"Yes."

We were pulling into our final station, Hiroshima. The Shinkansen came to a stop. I looked out the window, at the platform. Many passengers were disembarking from other trains. Then I noticed, they were all wearing black. Men in black suits with black ties. Women in black dresses with black scarfs. All were older. Many with canes and walkers. Some in wheelchairs.

I turned to speak to my fellow passenger, but he was gone. He was in line leaving with the others from our car. Like him, they were all dressed in black.

Then I realized they were all returning home, to Hiroshima. Today, August 6, on the 75th anniversary of the first atomic bomb dropped in war. They were survivors of that dreadful day.

I was standing on the platform when he saw me. He walked slowly towards me, steadied by his cane.

"I wanted to wait for you," he said.

"I'm glad you did," I replied.

"We are marching to the peace park to pray for a peaceful world."

"Oh."

"Would you ..." he stopped and looked in my eyes. "Would you like to join us, walk with me?"

I thought for a moment, about that afternoon meeting. About being punctual. On time. But then I remembered I was a Gaijin, a foreigner.

I smiled and then, without realizing it, I bowed slightly. It seemed so natural.

"I'd be honored."

THE LAST GREEN FLASH

"**D**on't get old, son."

He was sitting in his wheelchair. He was in his nineties. His grey hair needed a trim and a shampoo. His shirt was slightly stained in the front. Probably that soup we had at lunch, I thought.

"I'll try not to."

"It's the pits. Golden years. There's nothing golden about these years." He was angry and sad. I didn't know what to do, or what to say. Struggling to find words, I asked, "can I get you another cup of coffee."

"The coffee here is terrible. I think they're trying to kill us with it." A slight smile appeared. I guess he still has that sharp sense of humor, I thought, at least sometime.

"Perhaps tomorrow, a good cup of coffee from that coffee shop across the street. Can you do that?"

"Of course, I will, dad. Cream with two sugars."

"One, only one sugar. I have to control my diabetes you know." He looked to see if I noticed he was smiling.

"One it is. Are you ready to head back to the room?"

"Not just yet. I want to see that sunset. I think it's gonna happen tonight, just like those sunsets at the beach."

The beach. The smooth sand. All of us at the beach, when we thought it would never end. How could it? It was so perfect, every day.

My mother, my younger sister, my dad, and me. It was so, so perfect.

I was in high school. I would surf every day after school. On weekends we would have a family beach party with my dad's work associates. Colorful blankets spread out on the sand. Wine and cheese for them. Sandwiches and soda for the kids.

We would play together on the beach. Sandcastles, frisbee, and our parents would watch. Laughing, drinking wine, they would watch. In and out of that water, rendered so gentle by the curved retaining wall that stretched out into the sea. The occasional high waves stopped in their tracks by this imposing wall, which created, for us, such a tranquil setting on the other side. So tranquil. So perfect.

And then, when that time came, we would all stand. Facing west, watching the sun slide into the Pacific. Looking closely for the green flash. The adults would raise their wine glasses and then we would hear the horn which officially signaled that the sun had set. That it was gone for another day. But we had no worries, it would be back tomorrow to provide another display of colors, and if we were really lucky, a green flash.

The green flash. The first time I saw it, I thought this couldn't be. My eyes are deceiving me.

But it was true, it was green and a flash. A quick pop of green light, mere seconds, a small dot on the horizon just at the point where the last of the sun fell into the ocean.

Later, I learned that the green flash was caused by the sun's dispersion of its fading light through the atmosphere, in a manner similar to a prism. Conditions had to be perfect for it to happen. And when they were, and when it did, it was like the heavens were sending us a message.

We took that message as just the end of a perfect day with another perfect day to follow.

I know now that was not the message. It was really telling us to enjoy this exquisite moment, for who knows when there will be another. Or, if there'll be another.

On that evening, standing next to my dad, standing next to his damn wheelchair, we both saw the green flash.

"Perfect," he said. "The end of another day."

"Yes", I agreed, unaware it would be our last chance together for a green flash.

"Spinal stenosis," the doctors said. "Advanced. He needs to be careful that he doesn't fall."

And he was careful for a long time, but then one day he missed the curb. Landing on his face and into the hospital.

"Jesus dad, are you okay? Your face is a mess."

"Well, you should see the other guy." That smile again. It was a comforting smile. It always was.

From that day on, it was downhill for him. Had to move out of his house and into an assisted living home and finally to a nursing home. He hated it. And not just the coffee. "I want to go home," he would say every time I visited. I said I would look into it, but we both knew it wasn't going to happen.

The night of our last green flash, I got that phone call. The one I was dreading but expecting. You better get here.

I stood by the bed. He was motionless. Still warm to the touch. I held his hand, kissed his forehead. Stroked his grey hair. Told him I loved him. Over and over, I told him. Cried too, softly at first then uncontrollably.

The staff said, "we're sorry for your loss."

"I wanted more," I sobbed.

"What?"

"More green flashes with my dad."